All That Happens in the Dark

By July Waters

Copyright © 2025 by July Waters

All rights reserved.

No part of this publication may be reproduced, distributed, or transmitted in any form or by any means, including photocopying, recording, or other electronic or mechanical methods, without the prior written permission of the author or publisher, except as permitted by U.S. copyright law.

No identification with actual persons (living or deceased), places, buildings, and products is intended or should be inferred.

First edition 2025

Editor in Chief Samantha Nichols
Contributing Editor Misty Allen

Trigger Warning: The story you hold in your hands contains themes that may be traumatic for some readers. It includes topics of physical and mental abuse, arson, murder, the loss of loved ones, and grief. If these topics are of a sensitive nature for you, it may be wise to discontinue reading.

Chapter 1

It was quiet there in the dark. Silent except for her occasional sniffles. Her thoughts comforted her in this moment of isolation. She remembered her husband, how he had always taken care of her, how he was always soft and gentle with her.

They had married young. She was only 16. Her husband 18. Rumors swirled around news of their marriage. Very seldom do people so young get married unless there's a baby on the way. But there wasn't. Cheryl and Curtis were simply in love.

Cheryl and her mom planned a simple wedding ceremony at the church they'd attended since Cheryl was a baby. Curtis was happy to sit on the sidelines and let his bride plan the special day. She remembered prattling on about the colors of the flowers, and then she looked at him and saw that he was smiling at her. Listening to her bubbly chatter and smiling because he loved her so deeply. She was happy and that made him happy too.

She had chosen a plain white gown from a local mom-and-pop store. No lace, no frills. Just a simple A-line gown. She wore satin-covered flats to match and topped her ensemble with a traditional veil that covered her face.

"I remember, Curtis," she whispered in the dark of the closet. "I remember how lovingly you looked into my eyes as you lifted my veil..."

A loud noise from the living room jarred her from her sweet memories. It was Pete laughing at something he was watching on TV. The sickening sound of his laughter triggered more sniffles. It was the same laughter she'd heard when he shut her in the closet two hours ago.

Chapter 2

She'd been widowed. She'd waited a respectable amount of time before she began dating. Five years. Longer than most widows wait to find a new husband. Curtis wasn't one to be forgotten, and he'd left her with enough of his love to sustain her for a while. But she'd eventually reached a point where she longed for the comfort of a man's embrace again, so she downloaded a dating app and met Pete.

His profile said he was a teacher, and when she asked around, she learned that he was well-liked in the community. He loved building things and working on projects around the house when he wasn't busy teaching students. He was active in his church and was even part of the city's police reserves.

He seemed to be perfect.

She was trusting. She'd never needed to worry about how her husband had felt about her. He would never hurt her. He had worked hard to care for her, keep her safe, and give her all his love.

So, when Cheryl and Pete met for their first date, it was no surprise that she fell into his sticky web.

She'd never heard of love-bombing. She didn't even know that was a thing. All she knew is for the first time in over five years, a man was telling her repeatedly how much he loved her, how beautiful she was, and how they were soulmates.

"I have a modest house on an acre of land outside of town. It's in the countryside, a rural area with lots of privacy. The nearest neighbor is a few miles away. I love it there. I hope you will, too," he'd told her. "You'll be surrounded by nature and privacy. Even the gravel road out front is seldom travelled. It's very peaceful, Cheryl."

After five weeks of Pete's sweet words and promises, they married.

Chapter 3

Pete was a widower two times over. He'd never been divorced. From what he'd told Cheryl his marriages were wonderful.

His late wives had simply died and left him alone in the world.

It was something they had in common.

He and Cheryl had a simple, inexpensive wedding. Many guests attended, mostly Pete's friends and colleagues, and Cheryl's best friend and some distant relatives were there.

Cheryl had picked out and paid for her own dress. Being within a few years of proper retirement age, she opted for a neutral style she could wear on more than one occasion.

"Women my age shouldn't go in for frivolous things," she'd told herself when she picked up a bridal magazine at the hair salon and browsed the beautiful gowns displayed within its pages. "Practical is best."

Pete wore a faded pair of jeans and a button-down shirt he'd had hanging in his closet for two years. He completed his outfit with his best pair of cowboy boots, the ones he wore during the short time he dated Cheryl.

She pinned a white corsage on her dress, the same set of artificial blossoms she'd worn on her first wedding day. Pete wore a small boutonniere Cheryl had made using a bloom from a floral arrangement she had at home.

They had a basic reception in the church's fellowship hall after the ceremony. Cheryl's best friend had baked and iced a white cake, and Cheryl had made punch.

Their homemade wedding was less than inexpensive. It was cheap. That's how Pete wanted it.

"No use spending money when we already have everything we need," he'd told her.

Chapter 4

Two months into their whirlwind marriage, she planned a lunch date with her best friend. Cheryl was a social person, and they had lunch dates several times a month. She'd been without a husband for five years and received a substantial sum of life insurance when Curtis passed, so she didn't need to work. What better way to spend her time than dining and chatting with her closest confidante?

The first time she met Lorraine they were at the beauty shop. Cheryl was there for a trim. Lorraine was in the chair across the room getting her hair colored. Cheryl smiled when she looked at all of the foil squares in her color-treated hair. Lorraine looked up from her magazine at that precise moment and smiled back at Cheryl.

"It's amazing what it takes to look beautiful, right?" Lorraine had asked this stranger sitting across from her.

"We do put ourselves through a lot to look nice, don't we?" Cheryl had replied.

"Girl, I used to get all dolled up for the men. But men have let me down so many times, now I just get dolled up for me!" Lorraine said as she waved her manicured hand in the air.

Cheryl liked this woman, so she asked, "What's your name? Mine is Cheryl."

"I'm Lorraine! Nice to meet you, Hon!"

That day was the beginning of a deep friendship the two of them could have never dreamed up. They were so different from each other. Cheryl was simple and low-maintenance. Her hair was its natural mousy brown color. Her nails were trimmed short and unpainted. She wore no makeup, preferring the natural look.

Lorraine was all glam. Her richly colored brunette hair was distinguished by bold blonde streaks. Her nails were long and beautifully manicured, always polished in vibrant hues. And the jewelry! Every move she made resulted in jangling or clacking from her long, glitzy earrings and oversized bangle bracelets. She was Hollywood from head to toe.

Defying logic, these two unlikely friends became inseparable.

Lorraine worked as a clerk at a rice mill. She sat at a desk most of the day, flirting with the truck drivers who checked in with her when they dropped off their trailer-loads of rice. She enjoyed the attention, and the occasional invitation for a date, but she never got involved with any of the men. Certainly not the married ones, and there were lots of those who vied for her attention.

She worked the situation to her advantage, like any brilliant woman would do. She flirted, they flirted back, and then they brought her treats like burgers and sodas from the local truck stop. Lorraine cut the burgers into quarters, eating only one quarter at lunch, another quarter in the evening, and the same the next day until the burger was gone. She sipped the sodas slowly, not wanting to consume too many calories. And when the drivers brought her candy bars, she did the same. Lorraine had always been trim and willowy. She didn't want to ruin her figure in her later years. But she adored burgers and sodas! So, she enjoyed them within reason.

Cheryl wasn't overweight by any means, but she wasn't willowy like Lorraine. She wasn't strict about calorie intake. When Curtis gave her a burger, she would certainly eat every crumb in one sitting. No regrets. She was comfortably thick. She went for daily walks to stay healthy, but she'd never been concerned about looking slim. Her heart was happy and that's all that mattered to her.

"Hon," she said to Pete, "I've got a lunch date in town with Lorraine Friday. Just wanted to give you a heads up."

Pete had been working on cutting boards to make a birdhouse all morning. He had been abnormally quiet for several days, hardly speaking to Cheryl at all. She figured maybe things were difficult at work, or maybe he was having hormone fluctuations. Heaven only knows how often her hormones put her in a foul mood. She tried to give him a wide berth so he could deal with whatever had him so quiet lately.

He stopped in mid-saw and asked, "What do you mean?"

"Lorraine and I are getting together for a lunch date Friday. I wanted to let you know where I'll be," she explained.

"You can't do that," he said as he straightened his back and stared at her.

"Why not?" she asked. "You'll be at work, right?"

"Well… yeah," he said.

"Then there's no reason I can't go meet Lorraine," she said as she stared back at him unsure of what was happening.

She noticed his face was turning a light shade of red.

"Is his blood pressure up?" she wondered.

"No... I don't think it's a good idea," he said.

"And why not?" she asked.

He started to say something and then stopped to think.

Choosing his words carefully, he said, "It's not safe in town, Sweetie. How about we invite Lorraine over Saturday so we can both enjoy a nice lunch at home with her? I'd love to meet your friend."

"Why do you think it's dangerous for me to go into town?" she asked, thoroughly confused. "I have always gone into town by myself for girls' dates and I've never felt endangered in any way."

"It's just... it's just that I want to know my darling princess is safe by my side. That's all, Cheryl. I just want to take care of you and protect you. Tell Lorraine to come over at noon Saturday. I'll even help cook lunch, so you won't have to do it all by yourself."

"Wow, he loves me so much!" she thought as she smiled at him. "Of course, Darling. I'll call Lorraine in the morning and invite her for a Saturday visit."

"Call her now," he ordered.

"Now?" she asked. "It's ok. I can wait until tomorrow to call her."

"No, go ahead and do it now," he demanded. "Best not put off until tomorrow the things we can do today," he said in a sing-song voice. "No need to procrastinate."

He smiled, but there was something unnatural about it. Cheryl shivered, not sure why she had that response. While Pete was listening, she called and made arrangements for Lorraine to come over Saturday.

Chapter 5

Pete's idea of helping prepare the meal consisted of heating a pan of water to brew tea.

Cheryl slaved over pasta salad, tomato bisque, and turkey pinwheels. Once the main dishes were prepared, she mixed blondies batter and popped the pan in the oven for the vanilla brownies to bake.

The kitchen was a mess. Dirty bowls and silverware littered the countertops, and packages of cold cuts and shredded cheese were still out. And there were sticky-sweet tea splatters all over the stovetop and floor.

Pete had sequestered himself on the backyard patio once he'd finished the task of preparing tea.

Cheryl began to clean up. It was almost noon, and Lorraine was never late. She'd probably arrive early.

And she did.

Cheryl only had time to put away the cold cuts and cheese before the doorbell rang.

She wiped her hands on a towel, embarrassed that the kitchen was such a mess. Then she hurriedly walked into the living room to let Lorraine in.

She heard voices outside the door. Pete had come around to the front of the house to greet Lorraine before Cheryl could get there to let her in.

As she reached for the knob, the door swung open, and Pete guided Lorraine into the living room.

"Hey, girl!" Cheryl exclaimed as she wrapped Lorraine in a warm hug.

"Oh, my goodness! It's so good to see you, Cheryl! You know, this is the first time I've seen you since your wedding day! What's it been now? Two months?" Lorraine asked.

"It has!" Cheryl replied with a broad smile. "Two whole months since we got married!"

"Sorry to interrupt," Pete interjected, "but we have lunch waiting on us."

"Oh," Cheryl said. "Hon, lunch can wait a few minutes. Lorraine and I need to get all caught up on each other's lives first."

Lorraine looked at Pete and then Cheryl, confused by the rush to sit down to lunch.

"No, Honey," Pete responded. "We don't want to keep our guest waiting. We invited her over for lunch, not small talk. Follow me to the dining table, Lorraine."

Pete led the way, leaving Lorraine and Cheryl with nothing to do but to follow. When they made it to the dining table, he walked to the fridge and grabbed the pitcher of tea he'd made.

"Cheryl, bring some glasses, will you?" he requested.

"Umm... ok, just a sec," she said as Lorraine stood by the table trying to process the dynamics between Pete and Cheryl. Cheryl grabbed three glasses and brought them to the table.

"Get ice. We need ice," Pete said.

"Ok," Cheryl responded. "Give me just a little time. I can't get everything at once."

Pete stood and stared at her.

She grabbed an ice tray out of the freezer and popped ice into their glasses. Pete poured tea.

"I brewed the tea myself," he bragged to Lorraine. "It's a special recipe. Been in my family for three generations."

Cheryl paused as she turned on the faucet to refill the ice tray. She turned to look at Pete. He was busy pouring tea.

"He doesn't have a special recipe," she thought. "I saw him take the tea bag out of the box and plop it in the water. That's not a recipe. That's following the directions. What on earth is he talking about?"

For the first time in their new marriage, she rolled her eyes at her husband. She filled the ice tray and slid it back in the freezer.

As the trio sat down to lunch, Cheryl and Lorraine made every attempt at conversation, but Pete continuously interrupted them to talk about other topics. By the time the meal was finished, the two ladies still had not had a chance to have a full conversation.

Pete stood up from his chair and collected the dinner plates. He set them in the sink with the dirty bowls and silverware left over from preparing the meal. Then he approached Lorraine.

Placing his hand on the back of her chair, he said, "It's been so nice having you over! Let me get your chair for you."

Cheryl opened her eyes wide. So did Lorraine.

"Oh," she said as Pete pulled her chair away from the table so she could stand.

"Pete, we aren't done visiting yet," Cheryl said as she pushed back from the table.

"Well, we have things to do this afternoon. After all, it's a Saturday and weekends are short," he responded.

He stepped away from the dining area and headed to the front door of the house.

"It's been so nice having you, Lorraine. Please do come again soon," he said as he opened the door for her.

She looked at Cheryl. Then she hugged her goodbye and left. Pete closed the door, and Cheryl peered out the living room window at her friend getting in her car. Lorraine closed the driver's side door and sat there with the engine running for several minutes. Then she backed down the driveway and left.

Cheryl continued to stare out the window. Pete walked to the back door and stepped onto the patio. She didn't know what he was doing out there. Probably scrolling social media on his phone or reading one of his birding magazines.

Chapter 6

She walked away from the window and approached Pete as he sat in the metal patio chair, gently rocking back and forth as he read his magazine.

"What do we need to do this afternoon that's so important we had to make Lorraine leave?" she asked.

He ignored her and continued reading.

"Pete!" she raised her voice. "Why did we make Lorraine leave?"

He stood from his chair, tucked the magazine under his arm, and walked away from Cheryl and toward his woodworking building.

"Pete! Answer me!" she yelled after him.

As he walked away, she heard him mutter, "And so it begins."

She followed him to his shop and was trying to step inside when he locked her out. She walked over to the window and watched him. He thoroughly ignored her presence as he organized his tools on the shelf.

He used a whisk broom to sweep sawdust from his worktable and into a trashcan on the floor. Then he grabbed the broom and gave the floor a good sweeping. All while ignoring his wife who was staring at him from the window.

She got bored with trying to stare him down and began looking at his supplies. There was an entire collection of paint, from tiny cans up to five-gallon buckets. An assortment of used paintbrushes hung from pegs on the wall. On the floor beneath the paintbrush display were several gallons of some type of clear liquid.

"What does that label say?" she asked herself as she squinted and leaned closer to the window. "Hydrogen peroxide 50%," she muttered. "What does a woodworker do with peroxide?"

Chapter 7

She got tired of watching Pete and went back into the house where she called Lorraine.

One ring. Two. Three.

"Hello?" she answered.

"Girl, I am so sorry. I don't know what's gotten into Pete," Cheryl apologized.

"I have to admit, I'm a little disappointed and a lot surprised. That was very..." Lorraine hesitated.

"I know," Cheryl said. "It wasn't normal."

"You're right. It was *ab*normal," Lorraine concurred.

Just then Cheryl heard the patio door open. Pete was coming inside.

"I've got to go," she said. "Pete just walked in."

The two said a hasty goodbye and hung up.

Pete rounded the corner into the living room and asked, "Who were you talking to?"

"What?" she asked. She was sure they'd ended the call before he could hear.

"That phone call. Who were you talking to?" he said.

"That was Lorraine."

"She just left. Why did you call her right after she left?" he asked, his face beginning to redden.

Cheryl stammered, searching for the right words.

"I wanted to apologize," she finally said.

"For what? What did you do that you needed to apologize for?" he demanded.

"I didn't do anything to apologize for, Pete. I apologized for you."

"For me?! Why did you do that?!" he exclaimed.

"Pete, you ran her off! We didn't get to talk before lunch because you rushed us to the dining table and started pouring your tea. And then you made her leave as soon as she finished eating. You were so rude!"

He began to sweat. She saw a well-defined vein form on his forehead.

"There will be absolutely no more phone calls to Lorraine!" he shouted. "I will not be humiliated because my wife wants to badmouth me behind my back!"

"Wait a minute!" Cheryl defended herself. "You don't get to decide who I talk to and who I don't! Your behavior was rude, and if I want to apologize to my best friend because you were a jerk, that's exactly what I'll do!"

"No, you will not! I will not let you humiliate me! I pay the phone bill, and if you won't abide by my rules, I will cancel your phone!" he shouted.

She had never been in a shouting match before, certainly not when she was married to Curtis. Life with him had been peaceful.

"I have my own money, Dear. I don't need you to pay my phone bill," she said in the calmest voice she could muster.

He stepped closer. She had nowhere to go. The wall was behind her.

He reared back and slapped her phone out of her hand. Then he grabbed it from the floor and threw it against the wall behind her. She squealed and ducked. The phone fell to the floor in one piece, so he picked it up again, this time walking to the back door and onto the patio. He slammed it against the concrete pavers, then picked it up and slammed it down again. Then he grabbed the metal patio chair and placed the phone beneath one of its legs. He sat down in it and wiggled back and forth, causing the phone to shatter. In a matter of seconds, it had been destroyed.

Chapter 8

"Why did you do that?" Cheryl asked. "You broke my phone!"

"I did that because you have absolutely no right to disrespect me. And if it takes cutting you off from the rest of the world to teach you that, so be it."

Stunned wasn't the word. She was something far beyond stunned. The moment seemed surreal. She had never been treated this way before, not in her entire life! She didn't know how to respond to such strange behavior.

Pete skulked away, leaving Cheryl to think. She decided the wisest move she could make at that moment was no move at all. She would stay quiet and try to keep out of his way for the rest of the day.

Maybe he was simply in a foul mood and wasn't good at regulating his emotions.

"If I'm being honest with myself," she thought, "I don't know Pete deeply. We only know each other on a surface level. Maybe he just doesn't handle anger well. I don't think most people would have taken my call to Lorraine in the context that he did, but maybe that's just one of his quirks. Maybe I have a quirky husband. I'll just lay low and let him calm down. I'm sure everything will be back to normal by tomorrow."

She spent the afternoon taking care of household tasks and doing some reading. She smiled pleasantly at Pete in the moments when they made eye contact, but he didn't reciprocate. He glared at her and then went back to whatever he was doing. Cheryl couldn't make sense of it, but she enjoyed having a peaceful life, so she would do what she could to keep it that way.

That evening, she fixed a simple supper and pretended nothing happened.

As they sipped tea and ate their sandwiches, she mentioned, "When we get out of church after morning service tomorrow, we need to swing by the store and replace my phone."

Pete slowed his chewing and looked up from his plate. They made eye contact, and he smiled almost imperceptibly.

"I don't think so, Dear," he told her.

"Pete, I need a phone," she said. "If you'll recall, you destroyed mine in a rage fit. You need to make it right and get me a new phone today. And then never, *never* let something like that happen again."

"If I was in a rage, it's because of you, Cheryl," he quietly said. "It's not my fault you were running your mouth to your friend. That's all on you, Sweetie."

"You don't hold yourself responsible for your behavior?" she asked.

"I hold myself accountable for my behavior anytime I deserve to be held accountable. Today? No, you have to hold yourself responsible for your actions. *You* made the phone call. *You* talked bad about me behind my back, therefore *you* don't get to have a phone. The principal is simple. Or are you too thick-headed to understand that?"

He shoved another bite of sandwich into his mouth.

She was speechless. She couldn't think. She sat across the dining table from him appalled at what he was saying.

He finished his meal and took his empty plate to the kitchen sink. Cheryl continued to sit, her mouth hanging open.

As he walked away, Cheryl's brain kicked into gear.

"How dare he?! This is ridiculous! The man is off his rocker!" she muttered to herself. "How should I handle it? I've never been in a situation like this before."

As she thought of how to address Pete's horrible behavior, her mind drifted to memories of Curtis and their first fight.

"I could hardly call that a fight," Cheryl mused. "More like flirty arguing followed by a tickle war," she thought as she smiled. She remembered the moment as clearly as though it had happened yesterday.

She had painted their living room a warm shade of blush while Curtis was at work. She was pleased with her work and thought the room looked quite inviting. When her husband walked through the door that afternoon, the look on his face wasn't at all what she expected.

"Cheryl... you painted the living room without talking to me first?" he asked.

"Don't you like it?" she responded.

"Well, it's just that you didn't tell me you were going to paint the living room. I wasn't expecting it."

"So, you don't like it," she stated with tears welling up in her eyes.

"It's not that. It's just that I would like to be consulted too so I can be part of the decision-making process. That's all," he said.

"So, I have to get your permission to make choices?" she retorted with a touch of sass and a gleam in her eye.

Curtis looked at her and saw the look of mischief on her face.

"Why, you little devil!" he said as he dropped his lunchbox onto the sofa and swept her up into his arms. "You're trying my patience, aren't you?!" he laughed as he spun her around.

"Why, yes, Dear," she giggled playfully. "A girl has to see how much she can get away with!"

He gently tossed her in the oversized armchair and began to tickle her ribs. She squealed with delight as she struggled to escape.

"This is what you get for painting the walls without getting permission from the king of the house," he teased as he grabbed her feet and began tickling her arches.

"Oh, Curtis!" she spoke as she tried to catch her breath between spells of laughter. "That tickles! Stop! I can't breathe!" she giggled.

Curtis suddenly stopped tickling her and stood up straight.

"Cheryl, did you ask the landlord if we could paint?" he questioned.

She looked at him dumbfoundedly.

"I didn't even think of that," she said.

"Oh... that might not be a good thing," he said.

They stared at each other without saying a word. Then Curtis quickly reached for her and began tickling her again.

"Bye bye, rental deposit money!" he said as he continued his playful attack.

"We had good times," Cheryl silently consoled herself. Then her focus came back to the present and Pete. She didn't know what was wrong with him, but she felt compelled to get some distance and perspective. He had scared her. His behavior was suddenly not like him, at least not like the Pete she had married. This guy was a different Pete, and she didn't feel safe with him.

"I know what I'll do!" she thought. "I'll consult my women's Sunday school class at church! I'm sure the ladies will give me a place to stay for the day while I figure out how to tackle this situation with Pete."

The next morning, she showered, wrapped her freshly-washed hair in a towel, and popped a made-from-scratch coffee cake in the oven. While it was baking, she walked back to the bathroom and dried her hair. Once it was styled and she had applied her skincare products, she went to the kitchen and checked the progress of the coffee cake.

"Looks just about done," she muttered to herself. She turned off the oven and left the cake inside for two minutes longer while she started a pot of coffee. Then she took the coffee cake out of the oven and set it on the stovetop to cool.

She walked back to the bedroom to slip on her Sunday dress. Pete was sitting on the edge of the bed, hair disheveled, bags under his eyes.

"I've got a fresh coffee cake baked and a pot of coffee is brewing," she cheerily told him.

"Hmph," he grumbled, making no effort to move.

"Hon, we need to get going soon. You might want to start getting dressed," she encouraged.

His head swiveled to look at her as she shimmied into her simple blue dress.

"And just where do you think we're going?" he asked with a smirk.

"Church, silly," she said.

"Not happening."

She stood barefooted as she faced him upon his announcement that they weren't going to church.

"How come we're not going to church? Are you feeling bad?" she asked.

"Cheryl, are you completely stupid? I told you yesterday if isolating you from the rest of the world is what it takes to teach you some respect, that's what I'm going to do. Did you really think I'd turn you loose at church around all those other ladies you could belittle me to? Really?"

"Oh, come now," she gently said. "I'm sorry about yesterday. I love you dearly and will never risk saying anything again that might seem disrespectful. We have a wonderful relationship and I'm so happy with you," she lied, "I will never cross that line again. We haven't missed a Sunday yet. Let's not start now. We wouldn't want to be the talk of the church, would we? Or get a visit from the preacher this week because he didn't see us on Sunday?"

She hoped against hope that her sweet words would sway him. She was beginning to feel an urgency inside of her. Gut instinct was telling her she needed to get away.

"I said no!" he said as he raised his voice and stood up from his seated position at the edge of the bed. "What exactly do you not understand about the word 'no'? Maybe there's something else of yours I need to break to help you understand!"

"Ok," she stammered. "It's ok. Staying home sounds good to me."

She watched him as he walked to the closet to grab his clothes. She wanted to be sure he wasn't going to cross the room and hurt her.

Why was that even a thought in her mind? It was ridiculous. They were newlyweds. Why was she worried he might hurt her?

Chapter 9

Cheryl's health wasn't the best. She'd had a kidney removed years ago, and she took medicine to help the one remaining kidney work at peak capacity. She had days when she needed to take it easy, but most days she felt good and could tackle whatever life threw at her.

Pete was aware of her health condition before they got married. She had volunteered the information as they were getting to know one another. He had asked questions, like how severe the issue was, what kinds of medicine she took and how often, and if she ever had complications. She found his interest to be charming. It showed he cared.

Pete didn't have any medical conditions. He was healthy overall. No family history of medical issues, no daily meds, aside from vitamins and a single daily pill to help with blood pressure.

At least one of them was fully healthy. This thought comforted Cheryl. Neither of them was a spring chick anymore, and it was nice to know she would have someone by her side to help if her health ever declined.

Chapter 10

It was Sunday night. They went to bed at 10:00. Pete had to get up at 6:00 to get ready for work. Cheryl would wake early to fix his breakfast and pack a lunch.

She normally drifted to sleep soon after her head hit the pillow, but her nerves were frazzled tonight. He'd destroyed her phone and wouldn't let her go to church because he didn't want her to be in contact with the outside world.

But tomorrow morning he had to go to work. And she'd be home alone. She could drive her car to Lorraine's house and be safe from Pete and his desire to isolate her.

"Am I overreacting?" she thought. "It seems so dramatic to feel like I need to escape. But I do. I do need to escape. I married him too soon. We didn't give ourselves time to truly get to know each other. We rushed into it and now I'm living with a husband I find myself terrified of. No one should ever be terrified of the person they're married to. No, I'm not overreacting. I've got to get away from him," she decided.

She thought about Curtis and all of the lovely moments they had shared together. And how this would never have happened with him.

As she drifted to sleep, she thought about her nephew's wedding many years ago. Curtis and Cheryl both attended and stayed for the reception afterward. There was music, cake, and punch. Everyone was chatty and happy. And then the music started. The bride and groom had their first dance, then the parents danced with them, and then the DJ opened the floor to the others in attendance.

"If you're in love, I mean really in love, it's time for you to hit the dance floor with your partner," the DJ had announced.

Cheryl looked at Curtis, and he took her by the hand as he said, "I believe they're playing our song." He held her close as they swayed to the music. "I will love you until my dying day, Cheryl," he said as he looked into her eyes.

"And I will love you," she said as he guided her head to rest against his chest, "always, Curtis."

She was jolted awake by intense pain

"Curtis!" she shouted. "It hurts!"

She felt it again. A deep pain in her lower back. As her slumber shattered, she realized Curtis wasn't there. He couldn't help her.

Pete was lying behind her in bed, aggressively kneeing her in the small of her back.

"No! No! No!" she screamed in agony. "Stop! Please stop!"

One last thrust of his knee and he rolled away, apparently sound asleep. Cheryl couldn't breathe. The final blow had knocked the wind out of her lungs. She struggled to catch her breath, wheezing and gasping as she rolled over the side of the bed and went to the floor on her knees.

"What happened?? Did he hit me with his knee on purpose? But he seemed to be asleep, so maybe he was dreaming," she thought.

She caught her breath and stood up, bracing herself on the edge of the mattress. She stared at his dark silhouette in the bed and wondered if she should wake him. She decided against it. She didn't think she could handle another one of the rage fits that were becoming so common.

So, she stumbled down the hallway and into the living room where she curled up in the recliner with a throw blanket. Her spine popped as she shifted her weight to get comfortable, and the pain intensified. Tears rolled down her cheeks as she tried to keep her crying under control. She didn't want to risk sobbing too loudly and waking him.

She finally found a comfortable position and drifted off. Her sleep was fitful. She woke often throughout the rest of the night with a sense of dread nagging at her.

With her eyes closed and her mind dreamily playing out fictional scenarios in which she needed to escape a shadowy figure but couldn't, she heard Pete's loud voice saying, "Get up and get my breakfast, Sweetie. I have to leave for work soon."

She'd overslept. She dropped the foot of the recliner and began to stand when shooting pain dropped her back into her seat. She gasped.

"I can't do it this morning, Hon," she said as sweetly as she possibly could while trying not to cry from the pain. "My back is killing me."

"Seriously? A little backache is going to keep you from taking care of your husband?" he scowled.

"Pete, you hit me with your knee in my lower back repeatedly last night in your sleep. I'm hurt. I think I need to go to the doctor this morning. It's bad," she said.

"So, you're accusing me of beating you while you slept?" he questioned.

"No, of course not," she quickly replied. "You were asleep. You had no idea you were hurting me."

Why did she feel as though she was lying to appease him?

"You'd better not accuse me of something like that," he said. "It's probably that restless legs stuff. I get that sometimes. Both of my late wives complained about it. There's nothing I can do to stop it. I'm just a fidgety sleeper. Always have been."

"Oh, no," Cheryl responded without thinking. "That's not restless legs. My late husband had that. What you have is not the same thing. I never woke up with bruises when Curtis and I were married," she said.

"Don't compare me to your ex-husband! You're always talking about how much better he was than me!"

"*Late* husband," she corrected him. "I'm sorry it seems as though I'm comparing you to him. I don't mean to do that. But he's the only husband I ever had before I married you. He's all I know. I just don't understand how you can kick me so hard while you're asleep and you don't even wake up."

"Why are you so critical of me?!" he shouted as his face turned red. "You're always so critical!"

"I'm not being criti..." she tried to respond.

"Yes, you are!" he interrupted. "Shut up! Just shut up before I make you shut up!" he shouted as he glared at her with beads of sweat rolling down his forehead.

Cheryl took a slow step back. She wanted to ask him what he meant, but she was scared to say anything. Pete looked like he was about to explode.

She thought back to Curtis. He had always told her communication is the key to a healthy relationship. That and a lot of love. He had always encouraged her to speak her mind if there was anything bothering her. And when she did, he always listened patiently.

She decided communication was too important to stay quiet in this moment with Pete.

She straightened her shoulders and spoke up.

"What do you mean you'll make me shut up?"

He seemed to stand taller as he thrust his chest outward and came at her.

She quickly stepped back. And then another step of retreat as he lunged at her.

"I told you to shut up!" he shouted, droplets of spit spraying from his angry lips. "Shut up! Shut up! Shut up!"

He grabbed her arm as she tried to move away. He jerked, causing her to turn toward him.

"Pete! You're hurting me!" she screamed. "It hurts! Let go of my arm!"

He shoved her onto the sofa.

"Oh! My back!" she wailed as tears began to stream down her cheeks. "Pete, stop it! You're killing me!"

He stopped his assault and stood beside the sofa glaring at his screaming wife. Then he began to chuckle.

"Not yet, I'm not," he said so quietly that Cheryl wasn't sure she'd heard correctly.

Her screams faded away as she stilled herself on the couch. She sobbed and hiccupped, afraid to speak, afraid to move. She didn't make eye contact. She kept her gaze focused on the ceiling.

She could hear his heavy breathing. She felt his stare.

Her tears dried and the hiccups stopped.

Aside from the sound of Pete's breathing, the room was quiet.

How long had she been staring at the ceiling while Pete stared at her?

He moved. She flinched. He walked out of the living room, leaving her lying on the sofa. She heard the patio door shut. He was outside.

She rolled onto her side, wincing in pain. Being shoved onto the sofa had done a number on her back. She slowly dropped her feet to the floor and sat up.

She grimaced in pain as she walked to the bathroom to shower and process her interaction with Pete. She sat on the toilet while the shower warmed up, and she felt pain when she peed. There was a touch of blood in her urine.

"I've got to get to the doctor today," she muttered to herself. "My body took a beating last night with Pete's knee pounding me in the back. I feel like garbage right now."

She carefully showered and dressed, then eased down the hallway looking for Pete.

"Where is he…" she thought as she searched.

She found him sitting in a patio chair out back. She quietly slid the glass door open and told him she was going to head into town and see the doctor.

He was silent as he looked at her. His eyes seemed darker than normal. Maybe it was the soft morning light.

He looked away and pleasantly said, "No, the best thing for you to do is to stay home. I'll call the doctor for you when I get to work and see if there's medicine you can take to help. No need in you exerting yourself by going to town today."

"Pete, you don't understand. I'm in pain and there's blood in my urine. I only have one kidney. I *have* to see the doctor. This could be serious."

"Like I said, the best thing for you is to stay home. I'll contact the doctor for you," he responded.

He wasn't going to let her go to the doctor. But that was ok. She had her car, and she wasn't about to sit at home once he left for work.

"I'll grab breakfast and lunch at the school cafeteria today. And I'll call to let you know what the doctor says," he said, and then he smirked. "Oh, you lost your phone, you poor thing. I guess I won't be able to call you," he said as he walked out the door.

Chapter 11

She sat quietly in her recliner, listening to the sounds of his engine starting and his tires crunching on the gravel of their driveway as he backed out and into the road. It was 10 miles to the school, and it was already 7:50. His students would probably get to the classroom before he did.

She waited an anxious two minutes before she stood from her chair and peeked out the window. No sign of him. He was gone. She had all day to pack her stuff and leave, yet she felt rushed. She honestly didn't care if she took anything with her. She just wanted to get away and see her doctor before Pete could find out she'd left.

With that thought in mind, she brushed her teeth, ran a comb through her hair, threw on the first outfit she came across in her closet, and grabbed her purse. She headed for the living room, where she and Pete hung their car keys on the wall-rack beside the door.

It was empty. Where were her keys? She checked the floor and then the living room bookshelf. No keys.

"What did I do with my keys?" she mumbled as she searched beneath the couch cushions and under every piece of furniture.

A wave of terror hit as she dumped her purse onto the floor and rummaged. Where are those keys??

As she made her way to the bedroom and began to ransack dresser drawers, a realization hit her.

"He took them," she said aloud.

She stopped her search.

"He took my keys."

Chapter 12

"Now what do I do?" she asked herself. "I don't want to be here when he gets home. I don't feel safe with him. I can't be here when he drives up."

She began to weep and fell to her knees on their bedroom floor. She had forgotten about the back pain, but now that her adrenaline was bottoming out, she started to feel it all over again. She spent the rest of the morning on the floor, crying in fear and pain. Her thoughts searched every corner of her mind for a plan of escape.

But there wasn't one. Not without her car keys.

Chapter 13

"I could walk. I could take my purse and a bottle of water, and walk to the nearest house," she said to herself. "That's what I'll do!"

She carefully stood from the floor, grasping the handles on the dresser drawers for help. She walked to the kitchen, wincing in pain with every step. She filled a bottle with tap water, stuck a couple of granola bars in her pocket, and with her purse slung over her shoulder, she stepped out of the front door.

It was shortly after noon, and the day was warm. Grasshoppers fluttered across the lawn. Butterflies tiptoed across the rose blossoms in the flower bed.

And Cheryl took off walking across the yard toward the quiet, rural road.

Each step shot pain through her lower back, but she pressed on. She had no choice. She was afraid Pete would kill her. Was that unreasonable given his behavior over the weekend? Was she overreacting? No, she'd already had that conversation with herself. She wasn't overreacting.

"Restless legs, he said," she spoke quietly to herself. "That's not restless legs. Curtis had that from time to time, and he never kicked me or kneed me at that level of intensity in his sleep. Every now and then he would get fidgety. His legs might jerk a little. But then he'd get up and walk it off, and he was ok when he came back to bed. I don't believe for a second that Pete's knee repeatedly hitting me in my back last night was involuntary. There's no way."

Chapter 14

Her heart rate was up. Her adrenaline was, too. Now that she was moving in the direction of hope, her anxiety was through the roof.

"What if he comes home early and catches me?" she whispered to herself. "Just keep walking. Don't slow down."

But the pain was intensifying. That combined with the heat caused nausea to rise in her stomach. Sweat soaked the back of her T-shirt and the waistband of her jeans. Her feet ached. She estimated she had made it through the first four miles of her journey. Another four, give or take, and she would be at her nearest neighbor's house.

She heard the sound of an engine. She turned to see if there was a car approaching from behind. She didn't see anything. There wasn't anyone approaching in front of her. Where was that noise coming from?

"Geez, it's just an airplane," she muttered to herself as her heart raced.

Another mile in and she reached into her purse to pull out her phone and check the time.

"Dummy," she said to herself, "that's why I'm walking down the road right now. I don't have a stupid phone anymore."

She had no idea what time it was, but it had to be after 3:00. Pete would be leaving the school to come home around 5:00. She increased her pace as much as she could.

There it was! She could see the corner of the neighbor's yard. It was still quite a ways off, but she could see it. She was almost there!

She tried to jog, but she was hurting too much. It felt as though time was passing much too quickly.

A car. She could see a cloud of dust approaching from ahead. It was still a couple of miles away, but there was definitely a vehicle.

She ran. Pain or not, she ran with all her might.

And she made it!

She knocked and knocked, antsy about the approaching car, worried it might be Pete.

Her elderly neighbor answered the door.

"Hi, Mr. Jacobs. May I borrow your phone, please? Mine isn't working and I need to make a call. Would that be ok?" she asked.

He hesitated, unsure of why Cheryl had come all the way to his house to use his phone.

"How did you get here?" he asked. "I don't see your car."

"Oh, I couldn't find my keys, so I walked. It's such a lovely day for a stroll," she said, not wanting to unnecessarily alarm him.

"Hmph," he muttered as though he wasn't sure about the situation. "Yeah, come on in."

She stepped inside the house just as the approaching car rumbled by. She glanced behind her. It wasn't Pete. Thank goodness!

Mr. Jacobs handed her his simple flip phone.

"Oh, gosh..." she mumbled. "What's Lorraine's number?" Like most folks, she had no need to memorize numbers. She normally clicked Lorraine's name in her cell phone's contacts, and it instantly dialed.

For the life of her, quite literally, she couldn't recall Lorainne's phone number.

"I'll have to call the police instead," she told herself. "At least I can remember that number."

She called 9-1-1 and explained her situation to the dispatcher who answered.

"What's your address, Ma'am?" the lady asked.

"Well, I'm at my neighbor's house right now. I don't know his address. Let me ask," she said. "Mr. Jacobs, what's your address?"

He told her and she relayed the information over the phone.

"You say you're in danger?" the dispatcher questioned. "You believe your husband is trying to hurt you?"

"Yes," Cheryl said. "I know it sounds ridiculous, but he kept kicking me in the back while he supposedly slept last night, and he destroyed my phone, and he took my car keys. I just want to leave! Please help me!"

"Calm down, Ma'am. We'll send somebody out right away," the dispatcher assured her. "You say your name is Cheryl Jacobs?" she asked.

"No, no. It's Cheryl Adams."

"And what's your husband's name?" the dispatcher asked.

"Pete," Cheryl responded. "Please send someone out to get me before he gets home and starts looking for me!"

"Pete Adams," the dispatcher muttered. "Yes, Ma'am. Just sit tight. We'll get someone on the way."

Cheryl hung up and waited in the living room with Mr. Jacobs staring at her from beneath his bushy eyebrows. They didn't speak.

Five minutes passed… ten… fifteen minutes. She heard the sound of a car pulling up. Finally!

She glanced out the window.

Time stood still.

It was Pete. How did he know??

He jumped out of his car, slammed the door, and stomped onto the front porch. His fist thudded loudly and violently against the door.

Mr. Jacobs remained seated, his eyes big and his mouth hanging open.

The doorknob turned and Pete stepped in.

"Pete!" she said, trying to back away.

He saw Mr. Jacobs and immediately switched gears. His appearance softened. His voice was sweet.

"Cheryl, Darling," he cooed, "what on earth is wrong, Baby?"

He took a step toward her and extended his hand.

She stumbled over the coffee table as she took a step back.

He abruptly reached out under the guise of protecting her from a fall. He had her in his grasp now. It was over.

She crumpled to the floor and pleaded for him to release her.

Mr. Jacobs stood from his chair, staring at the situation unfolding in front of him. He cleared his throat and spoke.

"Pete, it seems like she doesn't want to go with you," he softly said.

Pete turned to glare at Mr. Jacobs, then caught himself before he lashed out.

With a forcedly gentle voice, he said, "It's ok, Mr. Jacobs. Sometimes she gets like this. She has some emotional troubles that we usually keep regulated with medicine. But Cheryl forgot to refill her prescription before she ran out of pills, didn't you, Baby?" he said as he turned his eyes toward her. "She will feel much better tomorrow after I pick up her meds for her."

Mr. Jacobs wasn't entirely convinced, but he didn't fight the situation. After all, this was Pete's wife. Not his. And it wasn't any of his business what the two of them had going on.

"Sure," Mr. Jacobs said as he stepped aside. "I understand how things can be."

Amidst Cheryl's pleas for help, Pete dragged her kicking and fighting to his car. He slung her into the passenger seat, buckled her in, slammed the door shut, and began to walk around the front of the car. Cheryl saw her chance to escape and threw the door open. As she attempted to jump out of the car, the seatbelt held her tight. She had forgotten to unbuckle. Pete saw her attempt at flight and stormed over to slam her door shut for the second time. Then he hurried over to the driver's side and got behind the wheel.

Mr. Jacobs was standing on the porch watching them leave. Pete forced a neighborly smile and gave a friendly wave as he backed down the driveway.

When he got his car aimed in the direction of home, he turned to glare at Cheryl. His face was red, and beads of sweat were rolling down his forehead.

"How dare you!" his voice thundered. "How dare you humiliate me like that!"

She stared out the window, listening to the rage in his voice, wondering what would happen when he got her home. She trembled as possible scenarios played out in her head.

"Did you think I wouldn't find out you had left me?" his voice boomed within the cab of the car. "Did you think poor, pitiful Pete would come home to find the house empty and you long gone?! You idiot! You embarrassed me in front of the entire town! Do you know who told me you were on the lam? Harold, that's who! The chief of police called to tell me dispatch had gotten a call from a frantic woman. *My* woman! Because of you I'm having to make up stories about how you're off your medication and that's why you ran off!"

Chapter 15

Pete berated her all the way home, but Cheryl didn't hear it. Her mind had drifted to thoughts of Curtis and the memory of the town's Fourth of July picnic during their first year of marriage.

The two of them knelt on a quilt spread on the ground at the far side of the park. She laid out sandwiches while Curtis poured from a thermos filled with icy sweet tea. They'd have a good view of the fireworks from their picnic spot.

They had sat and talked until daylight turned to twilight, and dusk turned to dark. As the cool of night set in and fireworks began to light up the sky, Curtis pulled her in close beside him and held her. They kissed, and then kissed some more.

The jolt of the car coming to an abrupt stop shook Cheryl from thought. They were home. Pete continued to scream at her.

She turned to look at him, no expression on her face.

"I want to leave," she said.

Pete stammered, "Well, what... well, of course you do! I just caught you at the neighbor's house trying to leave me without saying goodbye!"

"I need a doctor, Pete. My kidney is hurting, and I need a doctor," she spoke in monotone.

"Oh, you poor baby. You'll get exactly what you need!" he shouted as he jumped out of the car and charged around to Cheryl's side. He threw open the door, yanked her seatbelt away, and pulled her out of the car.

She had gone limp, her mind back on memories of Curtis.

He had begun working at a packaging plant after he graduated high school. He didn't make a lot of money, but it was enough. He wanted Cheryl to be able to stay home and be a homemaker. That's what she wanted too. Rent was affordable in their small town, so their single income was adequate to cover the cost of housing and food.

She spent her days cleaning and cooking, and every afternoon at 3:00 she began watching for Curtis to come home from work. She loved to see him pull into the driveway and step out of the car carrying the now-empty lunchbox she had packed full of goodies for him early in the morning.

He was always tired when he came home from work, but he was never too tired for Cheryl. His face broke into a mile-wide grin every time she opened the door to welcome him home. No matter how sweaty and dirty he was after a long day's work, she always had a warm embrace to give him.

"Oh, Honey..." Curtis told her, "I'm too sweaty and nasty to hug right now."

She wrapped her arms around him and pulled him close.

"That sweat is your sacrifice for our perfect life," she whispered. "It's dear to me. You're dear to me," she said as she began to gently sway back and forth. Before they knew it, they were moving in a music-less dance in the doorway of their rented home, with Curtis's lunchbox hanging from his left hand, and his right arm around Cheryl's waist.

Pete squeezed her wrists as he dragged her limp body across the yard. She wasn't resisting. She was no longer aware.

She was with Curtis.

They weren't overly outdoorsy types, but they decided to give camping a go. Curtis borrowed a tent from his brother, and Cheryl packed an ice chest full of sandwiches, potato salad, and a peach cobbler she'd made from scratch. They had set up camp next to a small stream in the national forest. They talked and laughed until midnight. Then they made love and fell asleep holding each other close. The next morning, they woke up covered in chigger bites. They were miserably itchy and ready to go home, but somehow they were having more fun than they could have imagined.

She was still locked in on this memory of Curtis when Pete deposited her into the backyard storm shelter and closed the door. He tromped over to his lawnmower that was parked under the shed a few feet away. He hopped on, turned on the engine, and raced to park the machine in front of the storm shelter door.

The sound of the mower just outside the shelter shook Cheryl from her reverie. She couldn't see anything. It was dark inside the storm cellar.

"Where has he put me?" she mumbled as she noticed the dampness of the space. "Am I... did he put me in the cellar?"

She saw just a hint of late-afternoon light near one of the door hinges. She put her face near it to peek out. A spider scampered across her arm, and she quietly shrieked as she brushed it away. Peering through the narrow crack, she saw the front right tire of the lawnmower.

"He's blocking me in?" she whispered.

She took a slow, deep breath and began watching to see what Pete's next move would be. He turned off the mower. She could hear his labored breathing. She caught a glimpse of his leg as he dismounted the mower and walked toward the patio. She heard the back door of the house slide shut behind him as he went inside, leaving her alone in the dark.

She began to weep. Then stopped. Her tears dried as she felt a sensation wash over her. It was the feeling of determination.

She pushed. She was able to force the door open about an inch. Not nearly enough room for an escape. But it was enough of an opening to allow daylight in. She continued pressing against the door and used the soft sliver of incoming daylight to check her surroundings. She'd never been in Pete's storm cellar before.

"What's that clicking noise?" she whispered to herself as she peered into the depths of the shelter. "Something's moving... what is that..."

She strained her eyes to locate the source of the sound, and she caught a glimpse of movement. Then more movement.

She gasped.

"It's the vent! It's the spinny vent thing on top of the shelter!" she excitedly muttered as she eased down the steps to investigate. She pressed her hands against the damp walls as her feet searched for each step. She made it to the bottom and looked up. The whirlybird was slowly turning in the outdoor breeze, drawing a hint of fresh air into the staleness of the shelter, and allowing muted flashes of daylight to penetrate the darkness.

She reached up to touch the base of it and instantly recoiled.

"Ick!" she softly squealed. "Spider webs!"

She reached up again, steeling herself against the possibility of touching a spider. She gently ran her fingers over the foundation of the turbine. Four rusty screws, one at each corner of the square base. Were they screwed into the concrete roof? She felt along the edges again. No, they're anchored into a wood frame.

"That wood feels a little crumbly, like it's rotten," she muttered. She pressed the pads of her fingers against it. The wood crumbled.

"Yes!" she whispered. "It's soft! If I can work the wood frame out from under the spinny thing, maybe I can knock the vent open and crawl out of here."

Whistling. She heard whistling. It was Pete. He was outside again. She stopped working on removing the whirlybird. She focused on the next step she'd need once the ventilation hole was open. She needed to find something to stand on so she would be high enough to shimmy out of the hole.

"What's this?" she whispered as she stepped toward the blocky outline of something on the floor. She reached down and examined with her hands. "Oh, water jugs. Probably not sturdy enough... wait! Water!" She hurriedly uncapped a gallon and took a long, drippy drink.

"Ick! That's been sitting there a while. Better than nothing though."

The mower cranked.

He was moving it.

Cheryl scurried back to the top of the steps and sat, seemingly helpless, at the door. She heard him drive away and shut off the lawnmower. Listening closely, she heard his footsteps thudding toward her.

"Cheryl, Honey, what are you doing sitting out here all by yourself?" he cooed as he opened the door of the cellar.

She squinted hard against the afternoon sunlight.

Pete left the door standing open and walked to the patio, leaving Cheryl sitting at the top of the damp steps, struggling to see.

It took several minutes to adjust to the fresh air and sunshine. She'd adapted to the dark, damp environment of the cellar quickly. She now found it difficult to get her brain and body to switch back into 'normal' mode.

She slowly got to her feet. She stood, breathing deeply, observing her surroundings. The woman who emerged from the underground shelter was not the same as the woman who went in.

She looked at Pete sitting in the shade of the patio. He was deeply engrossed in a video he was watching on his phone. And laughing.

She crossed the yard, one confident step at a time, and approached the patio door. As she reached to slide the door open, she felt a brief moment of fear.

She was standing beside him. He didn't acknowledge her presence. She slid the glass door open, stepped inside the house, and shut the door behind her.

She headed straight for the shower, feeling filthy after her time in the cellar. She caught her reflection in the bathroom mirror as she slipped off her clothes.

"Oh, my... I *am* filthy! Good grief!"

She stepped into the warm shower and slowly washed away the grit and grime of her unfathomable day. With body and hair thoroughly washed, she continued to stand in the shower so she could think without Pete disturbing her.

"I refuse to be trapped in my own home," she muttered to herself. "I absolutely refuse to be a participant in this circus Pete is creating! I've never seen such drama in my life! Well, except when I used to watch those stale soap operas while Curtis was away at work. Oh, my sweet Curtis... I miss him so much," she said as shower spray misted her face. Her body trembled as she stood there and let herself cry.

She remembered the day he died as though it had just happened. He'd been in a hurry to leave for work that morning. His stomach had been upset from some food truck tacos he had picked up at work the day before. Cheryl had packed his lunch, as usual, but he was craving Mexican. So, he indulged and later regretted it.

Cheryl stood by the front door holding his lunchbox and thermos. She was watching the clock and knew he'd be in a hurry to leave. She had the door standing open for him and snagged a quick hug and kiss before he sprinted off to work.

"I love you!" she had shouted after him.

He turned in mid-run and yelled, "I love you too, Cheryl! I'll see you this afternoon!"

She stood in the doorway smiling as he drove away.

She went about her daily tasks, cooking, cleaning, and she made a quick run to the library to check out the latest novel by her favorite author.

And then she waited.

But he didn't come home.

Half an hour of waiting, and then a familiar car pulled into the drive. It was Curtis's best friend and co-worker. Cheryl's heart sank. Something was wrong. Where was Curtis?

She stepped out of the front door and stood on the porch. Her brain told her to move, to walk toward the messenger in the yard, but her body wouldn't respond.

He approached and wrapped her in a firm hug. He held on and wouldn't let go until he had delivered the news.

His words seemed muffled, as though she was hearing him from the other end of a can on a string.

Curtis was gone.

Cheryl trembled in his embrace, unable to accept what he was saying.

"It was one of the machines. Curtis shut it down because something was stuck in it. He did everything right, the lock-out-tag-out, everything. But the new guy didn't know. He powered it up while Curtis was inside. I'm so sorry, Cheryl. So, so sorry," he said.

She crumpled as she whispered, "Curtis is dead?"

"Yes... I'm so sorry, Cheryl," he responded as he continued to hold her.

She didn't remember much after that. The rest of the day was a fog. Just an ugly shadow of a dream that couldn't possibly be real.

She sat in the porch chair the rest of the day and into the night. At some point, she didn't remember when or how, she went inside the house and curled up in Curtis's armchair. It was his favorite place to sit. It smelled like him. Like a hint of cologne with a touch of a masculine musk scent. She pulled a throw blanket over her head to trap her husband's smell inside so she could breathe it all in before it disappeared forever.

The next day was a blur. Curtis's boss and one of the owners of the factory came to Cheryl's house. They talked with her about the accident, but she didn't hear them. The grief was too loud.

She didn't call Lorraine. She didn't call anybody. She didn't think to. But somehow Lorraine knew. She showed up that afternoon to drive Cheryl to the funeral home.

The funeral director told her that Curtis's factory would be covering all expenses. There were no spending limits. She could choose the finest casket, the most extravagant floral arrangements, boutonnieres for the pallbearers, laminated bookmarks featuring Curtis's portrait and obituary - anything and everything she wanted was hers. All she had to do was say the word.

Curtis and Cheryl lived a simple life. She knew he wouldn't have wanted anything fancy. So, she chose a plain oak casket. She ordered a floral spray of wild daisies and ferns, two plants Curtis always seemed to enjoy. The director and Lorraine helped her write a brief obituary for both the newspaper announcements and the funeral bulletins – of which he sold her an order of 200.

"Would you like open casket or closed?" he asked her.

"I don't know. Closed, I guess. I don't know what I want. I just want my Curtis back," she mumbled through tears. "I want my Curtis!"

She cried deeply. The clerk slid a box of tissues across the desk. Cheryl clawed at the box, grabbing a handful of tissues. She angrily wiped her face, leaving it ruddy in the aftermath.

Lorraine put her arm around Cheryl's shoulders and gave her a little pat as she said, "It's ok, Honey. It's going to be ok."

Cheryl hiccupped, then breathed deeply and straightened her shoulders.

"I want a closed casket," she said. "And I want to be able to spend time with him alone before the funeral. I will want the casket open for that."

"We'll need you to pick out an outfit for his service," the director said.

"What? An outfit? What does it matter what I wear?!" she raised her voice.

"No, Sweetheart," Lorraine whispered. "He wants you to pick out a nice outfit for Curtis. Do you have one you can bring from home?"

"Oh... yes. I can bring one of his church outfits," she said.

"Very well," the director said. "If you could bring that by in the morning, we will get him ready for his home-going service."

Lorraine walked Cheryl to the car with an arm around her waist. She opened the passenger door and pulled Cheryl's seatbelt around her to click it into place. They drove away from the funeral home. Cheryl stared ahead in a daze. Neither of them spoke until they arrived back at Cheryl's and Curtis's house.

"Honey, are you sure you want to be here alone?" Lorraine asked. "I wish you'd come back home *with me, just for a little while, and let me make you some hot tea. Would you?"*

"Thank you, Lorraine, but I really want to be alone right now."

She walked inside the house as Lorraine backed her car down the drive. She shut the door behind her and fell into a sobbing heap on the floor.

"Why, God?! Why my Curtis?! Oh, God, I need him! I can't live without him! Please tell me this isn't real!"

She screamed and pleaded with God. Then she cried to the point where she couldn't catch her breath, and she screamed some more.

She spent the night in a puddle of sorrow on the floor. The same floor her husband had rushed across on his way to work the day before. The floor that witnessed their final goodbye.

"I love you too, Cheryl! I'll see you this afternoon!" he had said.

See you this afternoon...

She gave herself time to grieve. It seemed like all she had done for five years was grieve Curtis and the life they used to have.

She gave Curtis a final thought before she took a deep breath and refocused on the present.

"I'll stock the storm cellar with fresh water and snacks. Then stash a stool or something to stand on in there. I'll go out tomorrow and stow the supplies, and then I'll grab some of Pete's tools and loosen the turbine. That way I can pop it out easily next time he locks me in there. Yes, that's what I'll do."

She stepped out of the shower and toweled off. Then she wrapped a fresh, dry towel around her body and walked into the bedroom to put on her nightgown. She slipped it on and looked at her reflection in the full-length mirror mounted on the bedroom door.

"I look tired," she heartlessly chuckled. And then she noticed something. "What's that mark on my neck?" she whispered as she stepped closer to the mirror. She turned to get a better angle of light. "It's a spider bite!" she whispered in a panic. "That's the last thing I need…"

She stepped back into the bathroom and dug some antibiotic ointment out of the medicine drawer. She dabbed some on.

"That spot looks really bad," she mumbled. "I'm going to have to keep an eye on it."

She went back into the bedroom and grabbed an ink pen from her nightstand. Using the mirror again, she lightly marked the perimeter of the red area around the bite. This way she would be able to see if the affected area changed over the next few days. As she headed back to the nightstand to replace the pen, she had an epiphany.

"I can write a letter for help! I can send a letter to Lorraine!"

She was excited about this realization and could hardly wait for morning when she would have the house to herself so she could write it. For the moment, though, she had to settle down and focus on resting. She wasn't feeling well at all.

She quietly walked the length of the hallway and then rounded the corner to the kitchen. She filled a glass with tap water so she could take her evening medicine. As she turned the faucet off, she tiptoed to peek out the kitchen window. Pete was still sitting in his chair on the patio, deeply engrossed in whatever was on his phone.

She opened the cabinet where they kept their meds. Cheryl reached for her kidney medicine, but it wasn't in its usual spot.

"Where's it at?" she muttered as she began to rummage through pill bottles. "Where on earth is my medicine?"

She checked each pill bottle in the cabinet. Her medicine wasn't there.

"Pete..." the realization hit her. "But why would he do that? Why would he take my medicine? He knows I need it to keep the one kidney I still have functioning well."

She stood staring blankly into the cabinet, her mind whirring with possibilities. And then it became clear.

"He wants me to die."

Chapter 16

She stood staring into the cabinet, stunned at the revelation.

"But why would he want me to die? We just got married. He said he loved me. Why?"

She began to tremble as she stood frozen in place.

"Wait... he told me his other wives died too... but he never told me what happened to them. He said it hurt too much to talk about. I wonder... but why would he kill them? Why would he do something so horrific?" she thought. "Oh, Cheryl," she scolded herself, "you're blowing things out of proportion. That whole idea is ridiculous. Pete's not that kind of person. He's goodhearted. He loves me! And everyone in the community loves him! I'm being irrational because I'm stressed and exhausted. I just need some sleep. I'll be able to think much more clearly in the morning."

She was so utterly wiped out from the strain of the day that she didn't remember walking to the bedroom, or brushing her teeth, or slipping under the covers. She fell asleep immediately. It was only 7 o'clock.

It was a little after 10:00 when she awoke. Pete had gotten into bed. Her exhaustion gave way to adrenaline. There was no way she'd be able to sleep with him lying beside her. She lay still with her eyes closed, pretending to be asleep. He soon began to snore, and she carefully eased out of bed. She quietly walked down the hallway to the living room where she curled up on the sofa. She pulled a knitted blanket over her body and sank deep into thought.

"Start with the facts, Cheryl," she silently told herself. "Keep emotions out of it. What are the facts? What is actually happening?"

She grabbed a notepad and pen from the end table by the sofa and made a list.

- *Stole my medicine – maybe*
- *Shut me in the storm cellar, resulting in a spider bite*
- *Yells at me a lot.*
- *Won't let me be around other people*
- *Destroyed my phone*
- *Knees me in the back when I sleep*
- *Won't let me go to the doctor*
- *Took my car keys*
- *Lies to people about why I'm trying to get away from him*

"Geez... that's really bad. I wasn't overreacting at all. It just seems so surreal, like this awful life couldn't possibly be happening. But it is. That's it, plain and simple – it's happening."

She went back to planning her escape.

"I should stash water and snacks in the woods at the edge of the yard, too, in case I escape and need to grab some things on the go. If I can get away during the night, maybe I can walk all the way into town without being spotted. Once I get that far, maybe I can hitch a ride to Lorraine's house. I don't know if it would work, but it's worth a try. I don't think I can pull it off in the daylight though. Too many people might recognize me and report to Pete."

She was confident in her plan, and she was excited to get started.

"Come on, morning! I need to get Pete out the door and start on my prepping plan. And I need to get that letter in the mail to Lorraine. One way or another, I'm getting out of here."

She examined her bullet-point list again.

"It's just so ridiculous, it doesn't seem like it could possibly be real. Honestly, nobody would believe me if I told them Pete was treating me this way.

Especially not in this town where the community has him on a pedestal. Lorraine will never doubt me, though."

She heard him breathing. Pete was standing behind her looking over her shoulder.

"Is that a list? What are you writing?" he questioned.

Thinking fast, Cheryl responded, "I couldn't sleep so I'm making a to-do list for tomorrow. I hope my being up didn't disturb your sleep."

"While you're making a list, write down that you need to sweep cobwebs out of the corners. I noticed one on the bathroom ceiling yesterday," he said.

"Okay," she replied as she jotted it on her 'to-do' list.

Pete went to the kitchen to get a glass of water. As soon as he walked away, she tucked the list into the waistband of her panties and scribbled out a new one.

- *Wash sheets*
- *Weed flowerbeds*
- *Sweep patio*
- *Sweep away cobwebs*

She appeared to be deep in thought as Pete came back into the living room.

"Let me see your list," he ordered.

She handed it to him calmly, in spite of her trembling. Her quick thinking had saved her. Barely. If he had seen the real list, her punishment would have been severe.

He grunted as he handed the list back to her. He groggily retreated to the bedroom, leaving Cheryl alone with her thoughts.

She retrieved the original list from her panties, gave it one more perusal, and thoroughly scribbled out each word on the paper. Once she was sure her notes were completely unreadable, she slipped the paper under the couch cushion.

"I'll burn it tomorrow to be safe," she told herself.

She tried to relax. Cheryl desperately needed sleep, but she was afraid to let herself drift off with Pete just down the hallway.

In spite of her efforts to stay awake, she ended up slipping in and out of consciousness. It wasn't a good rest, but it was better than nothing.

She was jolted awake at the faint sound of Pete's alarm. It was time for him to wake up and get ready for work.

She got up and headed to the kitchen to pack his lunchbox. She quickly slapped together a sandwich, put a few baby carrots in a baggie, and tossed a handful of grapes in another. She added a snack-sized bag of potato chips, and his lunchbox was ready.

Then she brewed his coffee and poured it in his oversized tumbler. She placed a pre-packaged blueberry muffin on top of his lunchbox. Breakfast and lunch were ready to go.

She busied herself with cleaning the kitchen although it was already clean. She wanted everything about the morning to seem as normal as possible. She didn't want Pete to have any inkling that she had her own special plans for the day.

Ten minutes later, he walked into the kitchen, fully dressed and ready to go to work. As Cheryl stood at the sink washing dishes that were already clean, Pete walked up behind her, slipped his arm around her waist, and pulled her tight against him. He was squeezing her so hard she could barely breathe.

He leaned forward and whispered in her ear, "You'll be a good girl today, won't you, Baby?"

The sickening sound of his voice, his hot breath against her skin, made her want to vomit.

"I have my list of things to do today. Cobwebs will be gone when you get home this evening, Honey," she sweetly replied.

He grabbed his coffee and lunchbox and went outside. She heard the sound of his tires crunching gravel as he backed down the driveway.

He was gone. She had at least eight hours before he came back home.

Hopefully.

"First things first, I have to destroy the list I made last night."

She walked over to the sofa and pulled the crinkled piece of paper from under the cushion. She took a box of matches, stepped onto the patio, and burned the list.

"Now, I need to get a letter written to Lorraine," she muttered to herself as she stepped into the room they used as their home office. Well, Pete used the room. Cheryl never went in there. Pete was in charge of paying the bills, so he used the office each week to take care of that. Cheryl had never had a reason to go into that room. Until today.

She pulled out the rolley chair, sat down, and opened desk drawers until she found envelopes and stamps.

She began to write:

Lorraine, I need help! I honestly believe Pete is trying to kill me. I know it sounds absurd. Maybe he has a life insurance policy on me, and he wants to cash it in, or maybe he wants the money I have in the bank from the settlement on Curtis. I don't know why he's treating me so badly, but I need to get away. Girl, I need to see my kidney doctor, but he won't let me. I think he stole the keys to my car. I'm trapped here. And he destroyed my phone so I can't contact anyone. There's too much to say in this letter, but I am desperate for help. Please help me get away from him! Please, my friend! I need you!

Cheryl

P.S. Don't tell the cops! They're on Pete's side.

She folded the letter and tucked it in the envelope. She popped a stamp on it as she pondered whether or not to label it with her return address.

"No... better not do that. If for some reason it doesn't make it to Lorraine, it doesn't need to be returned to me. I can't take any chances on Pete accidentally seeing it."

She poised her pen over the face of the envelope, ready to write Lorraine's mailing address.

"Oh, good grief, Cheryl. Think! What's Lorraine's address..."

She knew it was Walnut Street, but she couldn't recall the house number. She'd been to Lorraine's house a million times, but the exact address wouldn't surface in her mind.

She stared at the desk, wracking her brain for the information she needed. Then she realized Pete's laptop was lying on the desk. She opened the laptop and turned it on. The screen came to life.

"Hmmm... I have to enter a four-digit code to get into this computer. Maybe it's his birthdate."

She entered the four digits of his birth month and day, but it didn't work. Then she tried the four digits of his birth year. That didn't work either.

"He bought this laptop the week after we got married. Our first 'big' purchase as a couple. Maybe he used our wedding date as his code."

She plugged in the date and the computer opened up!

"Wow! There are a lot of icons!" Cheryl said to herself. "Geez... why does he need this many?"

She had opened the computer to search the internet for Lorraine's address, but now she was captivated by all of the icons. She recognized some of them as being standard, but some were unfamiliar. One in particular stood out. It was an image of a set of binoculars.

She clicked into it and the screen filled with multiple videos playing all at once. She stared at the first one, then the second, and third... it was live security camera footage of a yard. Their yard.

She gasped as she whispered, "I've been under surveillance!"

She continued to view each live video and realized there were cameras in the house too. She had never seen a camera. How was he getting all of this security footage?

She made mental notes of what parts of the yard and interior of the house were being watched and then stepped out of the office to search for the cameras.

"They must be miniscule! I don't see cameras anywhere!" she mumbled as she searched the living room.

And then she found the first one. It was tiny. Smaller than a double-A battery. It was tucked between magazines in a stack of old police publications on the bookshelf.

"So, that's it. They're mini-cameras. And they're all over the place," she whispered. "This puts a damper on my plans to stash supplies outside. I wonder if I can get my letter to the mailbox without the cameras picking it up."

She went back to the laptop, grabbed a sheet of paper, and made a rough map of the property and which areas were under surveillance.

"At least he's not watching me in the bathroom. But the living room, kitchen, bedroom... and the office! Good grief, what if he's watching me right this second?!"

She hurriedly looked over her map again.

"I think I can get my letter to the mailbox without getting caught. I'll tuck it in my pocket when I go out to weed flowerbeds. Then I'll casually work my way out of sight and to the mailbox. Oh! I still need to look up Lorraine's address!"

A quick search turned up the information she needed. She put Lorraine's address on the envelope, tucked it in her pocket, and started to shut down the computer.

"Wait, I need to wipe the history…" she mumbled. She had to do an online search to get a tutorial on how to wipe the history without disturbing Pete's stuff.

She removed all traces that she'd used the computer, then shut it down and walked out of the office. As she pulled the door shut behind her, she stopped.

"This is how Pete knew I was on the phone that day. The cameras must send videos to him on his phone. That's the only way he could have known I was making that call. He's been watching every move I make!" She hoped with all the positive energy she had that Pete was busy teaching his students and didn't know she was in his office.

Feeling a pressing sense of urgency, she focused again on the task at hand. She put on her yard shoes and gardening gloves. Then headed out to weed the flowerbeds. After several minutes of authentic weeding, she worked her way to the mailbox and put the letter inside. Just in time too. She could see the mail carrier driving in her direction on the quiet rural road.

"Maybe I should talk to her and tell her what's going on. Maybe she could help me," she thought. And then she decided against it. "I don't know who's connected to Pete and who would turn against me. It's safer to keep quiet. Lorraine will help me. I just have to survive until my letter makes it to her."

Chapter 17

After her letter had been safely deposited in the mailbox, Cheryl wandered around the yard picking up limbs. She wanted to be sure Pete's surveillance cameras showed her working hard on the lawn.

20 minutes passed. She was sweating from her labor and went into the house to get a glass of water and consider what her next step should be. As she stood in the cool air of the kitchen, she decided it was time to start stashing supplies around the property.

"I think I can conceal what I'm doing if I get on the lawnmower and ride around the yard... Yes! This will work! I'll put the five-gallon bucket on the mower like Pete does when he mows. I'll occasionally toss a limb into the bucket, like I'm using it to collect yard debris, but I will actually have supplies inside the bucket so I can deposit them in strategic locations. This will absolutely work! He will look at his surveillance footage and simply see his wife hard at work maintaining the lawn. It's a perfect plan!"

She stepped out of camera view and pulled out the rough map she had drawn.

"Looks like the lawnmower shed is being watched. And the patio too. What if I drop supplies out of the kitchen window and then ride the mower over to pick them up? The edge of the house at the window isn't targeted. I think I can do that. Now... what supplies should I take?"

She rummaged through the utility room cabinet. It was filled with cans of wasp spray, boxes of nails, hammers, screwdrivers, and loads of other small tools. Cheryl grabbed a handful of miscellaneous tools and a couple of cans of wasp spray. Then she hurried back to the kitchen, slid the window up, popped out the bottom corner of the window screen, and dropped each item out individually.

Then she grabbed four bottles from the cabinet and filled them with tap water. She lowered the filled bottles out of the window as carefully as she could so they wouldn't get damaged when they hit the ground. Next, she grabbed a handful of granola bars and packs of trail mix from the snack cabinet. She dropped those out of the window too.

"I think I'm ready to get back outside now," she said to herself in a silent pep talk. "Here I go!"

She stepped onto the patio, knowing the camera was watching her. She walked casually to the lawnmower shed, where another camera was now watching. She grabbed the lawn bucket, cranked the mower, backed it out, and started mowing the lawn.

She began mowing in the same pattern Pete always used. Edges first, which was perfect because she needed to drive next to the house and pick up all the supplies she had dropped from the window. As she made her first pass by the house, she stopped the mower and quickly reached down to grab the supplies. She tossed them in the bucket and began driving again. The whole action had taken about ten seconds. Maybe Pete wouldn't notice she had been out of frame for too long.

She continued to mow and occasionally stop, within range of surveillance cameras, and toss limbs into the bucket. As she neared the edge of the yard, where the woods began, she made a quick movement to toss a water bottle and a couple of snack bars behind a large oak tree. Then she tossed a screwdriver too.

She tossed a hammer behind a tree a little farther along, and a can of wasp spray and a bottle of water with it.

"Heaven forbid I need to use a hammer or screwdriver in self-defense. How gory! Of course, using the wasp spray in self-defense seems harsh too. But if it's my life or his..."

She continued driving the mower, realizing that the remaining supplies all needed to go in the storm cellar. That was going to be a challenge. The cellar was under surveillance.

"How am I going to get into the storm shelter without Pete seeing me on the video?" she mumbled as grass and dust whirred around the mower.

"The only thing I can think of is to disable the camera. Or shift its angle. I'll have to find it before I can do anything."

She made round after round with the mower, searching for the tiny camera every time she passed near the house. It had to be mounted somewhere near the patio. She searched but couldn't locate it from the seat of the lawnmower.

"I'll have to use a different tactic to find it," she thought. "I have an idea that might work... I'll park the mower in the yard and make it look like insects are swarming me. Then I'll take a can of wasp spray around the house and pretend to spray bugs. Maybe I'll be able to find the camera that way. And I can coat it with spray to fog it up. It will look completely innocent."

She walked the perimeter of the house, occasionally squirting wasp spray near the eaves, even though there were no wasps there. She needed her activity to look authentic. When she got near the patio, she spritzed a little spray here and there, acting like she had found a swarm of bugs. Her eyes strained, searching for the black shine of the camera lens.

"There it is!" she realized, without saying a word. She swatted her hands in the air as though she was fending off wasps, and then she sprayed a heavy coating of poison on the camera that was neatly wedged in a hollow spot between two bricks in the wall. While the lens was dripping with spray, she bumped it gently with her hand, causing the angle to change just enough to aim it to the right of the storm shelter.

"Now, I can stash stuff in the cellar without being seen," she congratulated herself.

She continued around the house, pretending to spray bugs. When she was finished, she went back to the mower, cranked it up, and made another pass across the yard. When she neared the cellar, she parked the mower, jumped off, and grabbed the remaining water, snacks, half-used can of wasp spray, and tools. She threw the door open, trotted down the steps, and laid the supplies in a corner. Then she headed back above ground, closed the door, and pretended to continue to do yard work with the mower.

Once she had parked it in the shed, she went into the house to wash her hands and arms and get a drink. Sweat was getting in the spider bite causing it to burn. She grabbed some ointment from the medicine cupboard and dabbed it on. Then she went back into the yard with the rake and pretended to rake grass clippings away from the flowerbeds and edges of the house. Once she was out of the line of vision of the cameras, she went back into the cellar and began to loosen the turbine vent with the tools she had dropped off earlier.

"Just one more screw to loosen," she muttered as she worked. "There! All the screws are out. Now, let me see if I can wiggle it out of its hole in the ceiling… Yes! It's free! Ok, calm down, Cheryl. You've got to make it look like it's still secured in place."

She nestled the unfastened vent back into its spot in the ceiling, confident that she could pop it right out to escape the next time Pete locked her up.

"Now, how can I get high enough up to crawl through that space?" she pondered. "I need something to stand on, something that would look innocent enough if Pete found it down here."

She walked out of the shelter and into the bright light of day. She squinted against the sunlight as her mind mentally coursed over the property. There must be something she could use.

"Wait!" she excitedly whispered. "The bucket! I can turn the five-gallon bucket on end and use it for a stool. And it will look perfectly at home in that dark cellar. Now, how will I get it there?"

She got back on the mower and acted like she was mowing, although the yard was already as smooth as a golf course. As she passed by the storm cellar, she braked, opened the shelter door, and tossed the bucket down the steps. She let the door fall shut and then she continued toward the shed to put away the machine for the second time. Once she got it parked, she dismounted, dusted the grass from her jeans, and mentally congratulated herself on a job well done.

Chapter 18

Having finished her tasks, she retreated to the cool of the house to get a shower and put on some clean clothes. She disrobed from her dusty work clothes and tossed them in the washing machine. Then she made a quick walk down the hallway and to the bathroom. As the shower water was warming up, Cheryl looked at herself in the mirror.

She leaned in and said, "You're getting out of this, Cheryl. This is no way to live, and it's no way to die. You *will* get out of this."

She noticed the spider bite. She had forgotten all about it.

"Wow, it looks worse. I can't see the pen marks anymore, though. I must have sweated the ink off. But it doesn't matter. I can see the infection is spreading. And the puncture marks are becoming more defined."

She showered and dressed with only an hour left until Pete's arrival home after work. She needed to cook his supper. She wanted him to be as happy as possible this evening. Her day had been challenging enough without the possibility of facing Pete's rage before bedtime.

She dabbed some ointment on the spider bite and covered it with a bandage. Then she headed to the kitchen to whip up something for supper.

By the time Pete got home, his meal was steaming hot and waiting for him on the dining table. He slipped off his shoes by the front door and focused on Cheryl. His stare was cold. His face showed no emotion. Then his lip twitched and his forehead wrinkled.

"What's that on your neck?" he asked.

"Oh, that's a bandage. I have a spider bite. It's become infected and looks bad. I put some ointment on it and covered it," she explained, as though having a poisonous lesion on her neck was normal.

"Oh, yeah," he said. "I remember seeing that bite. You should probably go to a doctor and get some medicine for that," he said as he chuckled. "It *could* kill you, Baby," he stated in a syrupy sweet voice as he walked toward the bathroom to wash up for supper.

"It's exactly what I thought," she told herself. "He wants me to die, and he wants it to look natural. I don't know why for sure, but that's definitely the goal he's working toward. With that being the case, he will keep me here and away from other people until I'm dead."

Chapter 19

Just as she completed her thought, she heard Pete slam the bathroom door and stomp toward the dining room. When he rounded the corner, he glared at Cheryl.

"His face is red. He's sweating. Something bad is about to happen," she thought quietly as she braced herself.

"What did you do today?!" he blustered. "What did you do?!"

"Does he know what I did?" she secretly questioned herself. "There's no way he could know..." She steeled her nerves and calmly replied, "What do you mean, Honey? I cooked and cleaned today."

"You cleaned?" he scoffed. "You *cleaned*?! Then why are there still cobwebs in the bathroom?! I specifically told you to sweep away the cobwebs! You were home all day! Why didn't you do as you were told?!"

"Oh, my gosh... I forgot about the cobwebs... I'm so sorry, Pete. I'll clean them right now. You go ahead and have your supper. It won't take me long," she encouraged. "Won't take me long at all."

"Nah," he said. "You had plenty of time to work on that today! You wanted me to be mad! You wanted to see how angry you could make me by disrespecting me again! You like to disrespect me, don't you?! I don't know how that Curtis ever put up with you and your nonsense!"

"Don't you dare utter my husband's name!" she responded.

"Your *husband*?!" he shouted. "*I'm* your husband!"

He grabbed her wrist and began dragging her toward the patio door. Out they went, with Cheryl screaming and thrashing. He dragged her across the patio pavers, the yard, and tossed her down the storm cellar steps.

"Maybe it's time you learn to respect your man!" he shouted as he slammed the shelter door.

She lay in a heap at the bottom of the steps until she heard his mower crank up. She sat up and listened, waiting for him to park it in front of the door. When he blockaded her in, he killed the engine, and walked away, shouting obscenities.

"I wish the people at church could see this upstanding citizen right now," she thought as she checked herself for possible broken bones. "I don't think anything's broken, but I'm definitely scuffed up and bleeding."

She situated herself on the bottom step to sit and think.

"Last time I don't think I was barricaded in the shelter for very long. Maybe half an hour. It could have been more. I'm not sure. I wonder if it will be the same this time. I'd like to make my escape when it's dark. I'm sure he will see me if I try to shimmy out the vent hole in broad daylight."

It was around 4:00, a long time until sundown.

"All I can do is sit and wait. And eat a granola bar," she smiled as she gingerly stood and walked to her stash. "I refuse to sit here and get weak from hunger if I don't have to. Pete doesn't hold all the cards in his little cat and mouse game."

Chapter 20

An hour passed. Then two. He hadn't come back. Cheryl was getting her hopes up for a nighttime escape.

But he showed up at dusk, just in time to let Cheryl out and then go to bed.

"It's a shame you fell down those steps," he said. "You're all scraped up. You've got to be more careful, Baby."

He walked ahead of her and went inside. Cheryl stood just outside the cellar door for a while to collect her thoughts.

"This spider bite is starting to hurt," she mumbled as she ran her fingers across the bandage. "Should I try to run away after he goes to bed? I don't feel so good all of the sudden. Maybe it's just because I've had such an exhausting day."

She quietly walked in the house and realized Pete had already tucked himself in for the night. Cheryl checked the medicine cabinet. Still no pills.

She resigned herself to a warm shower in the guest bathroom and another night on the sofa. She couldn't make herself lie next to Pete. There's no way she could sleep in the same bed as him.

She showered and checked the spider bite in the mirror. It was worse. The red streaks were very pronounced. The longest one looked to be over two inches. The puncture wounds had turned into small craters, dark with the rot of poison. It was a brown recluse bite. Very hard to cure, even with the help of a doctor.

"I've got to lie down," she told herself as she headed toward the living room. "I don't feel well at all."

She settled on the sofa and wrapped up in a blanket. She fell asleep instantly.

She slept the whole night through without even needing to wake up to use the bathroom. She could hear Pete's alarm going off. It was time to get up.

She eased off the couch, still tender from being dragged across the yard yesterday. She went into the kitchen and started the coffee. As she packed his lunch, her mind went to work.

"He won't kill me yet. I have too many bruises and scrapes. People will question him about my condition. He has to wait until I'm healed before he can kill me in such a way that looks natural. I have time."

Her thoughts comforted her to a degree. But the feeling of urgency never left.

With his lunchbox in one hand and his coffee tumbler in the other, Pete walked out the door and left for work without a goodbye. That was fine with Cheryl. She was tired of pretending to be a happy wife.

"Twice he has locked me in the cellar, and twice he has let me out before dark. Escaping under cover of nightfall might not be an option. What other options are there? Oh! I almost forgot about Lorraine! She will come to save me! But I can't wait for her. Pete's temper is so volatile. Maybe he will let me live until I heal, but maybe he won't. I still need an escape plan."

She went to the bedroom to dress herself for the day. Once she was dressed, she walked to the living room and sat down to think.

"Oh! I have an idea! What if... I tell Pete tomorrow morning that I'm feeling really bad... and I want to take a long, hot shower? I can get up early and fix his lunch, so nothing seems out of the ordinary. While he's getting ready for work, I can turn on the guest bathroom shower and lock the door. It will sound like I'm in the shower, but what I can do is sneak out to his car and hide in the trunk! Once he gets parked at the school, I can pop the hatch and slip out! That's it! That's what I'll do!"

She rolled over the details of the plan searching for any reason it might not work. She couldn't think of anything that could go wrong. He wouldn't be watching his cameras while he was busy dressing for work.

With her failproof plan in mind, she felt at peace. She spent the day sleeping on the sofa. Sunlight hit her eyes a little after 2:00 as the afternoon sun shone through the window.

"I'd better get up and start cooking supper. I don't want Pete to have any reason to be angry tonight. It would be nice to have a quiet evening for a change."

She set about preparing meatloaf, green bean bundles, mashed potatoes, and corn on the cob. Once a week she cooked a dessert. She figured tonight would be a good night to round out dinner with a sweet treat.

"If his stomach is full, maybe he will be happy and go to bed early," she hoped.

She set the table and waited for him to come home. She was feeling ill again.

Just then she heard Pete's car drive up.

"That's the lovely sound of my upcoming ride to freedom," she sighed.

Pete trudged in, looking tired and disgruntled. Cheryl was disgusted by the sight of him, but she had a performance ahead of her, so she painted on a fake smile and forced a lilt to her voice.

"I'm so glad you're home, Honey," she cheerily said. "I've missed you. How was your day?"

He ignored her, kicked off his shoes, and went to the bathroom to wash up. He was silent when he came back and sat at the dining table. Cheryl was fine with that. She really didn't have the strength to force herself to be sweet.

They ate their meal in silence. Pete shoveled large portions of food into his mouth, finishing up with dessert. He was stuffed. She was sure of it.

He pushed back from the table, gave Cheryl a cold glance, and then retired to his recliner. He turned on the TV and fell asleep.

"Well, I wasn't expecting him to fall asleep in his chair," Cheryl thought.

She washed dishes and cleaned up the kitchen as quietly as she could. She didn't want to wake the beast. She enjoyed the quietness of the evening.

When she finished her work, she eased out of the patio door and took a seat in one of the rockers.

"My ankles are swollen," she noticed. "I'm retaining fluid. When is the last time I peed?"

She rocked in the chair on the patio until almost bedtime. Then she went inside to find Pete still asleep in the recliner.

"I can't wake him. It's been a nice evening. I don't want him waking up in a rage. How am I going to carry out my plan tomorrow with him sleeping in his chair right by the door?"

She realized all she had to do was make her getaway while he was getting dressed. A wave of relief washed over her.

"Now, where am I going to sleep? I don't want to be in the living room with him," she thought.

Just then Pete stirred. His eyes opened and he saw Cheryl staring at him.

"Why are you looking at me?" he questioned.

"I was just wondering if you're comfortable in your chair," she said.

"Yeah. I'm going to go to bed though. I've been in this recliner long enough," he said.

"I'm not tired yet, so I may stay up a while. Sweet dreams, Darling," she said as he walked away.

She smiled knowing this would be the last night she'd spend in the same house as him.

Chapter 21

She slept fitfully on the sofa and woke to the muffled sound of Pete's alarm coming from the bedroom.

"I'd better hurry!" she thought as she shuffled to the kitchen to put together his lunch and coffee. Once she had everything ready for him, she hurried to the bedroom where he was almost finished getting dressed.

"Good morning, Hon," she said. "I'm not feeling well this morning. I'm going to get a long, hot shower. Your lunch is on the kitchen counter ready to go."

"Hmph," he responded as he slipped on his socks. Then he looked at her and smiled. Not a warm smile, but a cold one.

"I guess he thinks I'm on death's doorstep," she thought. "He makes me sick."

Cheryl hurried to the bathroom and turned on the shower. She turned the lock and pulled the door shut.

"Perfect!" she thought.

She slipped on her yard shoes that were by the front door, and she quietly stepped outside. She made a dash for Pete's car. She opened the door and pulled the latch to pop the trunk open. She glanced at the front door to be sure she wasn't being watched. After she silently pressed the car door shut, she scurried into the trunk. She fumbled for a moment but was finally able to pull the trunk lid closed. She had successfully shut herself inside Pete's trunk.

It was stiflingly hot in there. But it wouldn't last long. She'd be back out in the fresh air as soon as he got to work.

She was nauseous. She wasn't sure if it was the adrenaline or the infection.

After an eternity of waiting, she heard the car door open. The car rocked from side to side as Pete situated himself in the driver's seat.

"He's in!" she mouthed to herself.

The engine cranked. The car shifted into reverse. They were backing out of the driveway.

She felt the car stop rolling. Then it began going forward. The sound of the tires humming along the road comforted her. She was close to freedom and help.

The car hit a pothole and was jarred. Cheryl bounced around and forced herself to stifle a moan of pain. They hit another bump in the road, and the trunk lid bounced open a bit. Cheryl quickly grabbed it from underneath and brought it back down into place.

"I thought I had it latched! Oh, my gosh... if Pete saw the trunk come open... he'll kill me!"

The car slowed but didn't stop. Pete continued driving. Cheryl held onto the trunk lid with all she had. She couldn't risk letting it pop open again.

After several minutes of sheer terror, she felt the car turn, and turn again, and then come to a stop. She could hear the chatter of kids. They were at the school.

She heard the sound of Pete's briefcase sliding across the front seat of the car. He slammed his door shut and clicked the fob to lock the car. She heard his footsteps crunching on the gravel parking lot as he walked away.

"I made it! It worked!" she silently cheered.

She continued to lie still, waiting until class started and Pete was behind his desk. She didn't want to exit the trunk too soon and risk someone seeing her and reporting to Pete.

She listened to the footsteps of other staff members as they parked and walked by her hiding spot. It felt odd to be so close to help yet so far. She knew she couldn't reach out to them. Pete had a hold on the people of this community. She was certain his colleagues would stand by him no matter what she told them.

More footsteps, this time approaching the car instead of walking past. The trunk flew open!

"Wha.. what?!" Pete stammered as he discovered his wife balled up in a sweaty mess in the trunk of his car. "What are you doing?!" He caught himself and checked the parking lot to see if there were witnesses. It looked like everyone had already made it into the building.

"You're so adorable back here, Cheryl," he mocked. "You thought you'd sneak away, did you? How is that working out for you?" he sneered. "I'll hand it to you, you almost made it. That was a pretty clever idea, Baby."

He slammed the trunk lid closed and got back in the driver's seat. He cranked the engine, but the car didn't move. Cheryl began pounding the lid of the trunk and screaming for help, but there was no one to hear her. Between her screams, she could hear Pete talking. He had called in to tell the superintendent he was running late because his wife was sick. He would get to work as soon as he could.

"He's taking me home."

Chapter 22

She mentally braced herself. The punishment would be severe. She had almost escaped, and he would be sure to hurt her.

The drive home was much rougher and curvier that the trip into town had been. He was driving erratically with the intention of injuring her. And it was working. By the time he parked in the driveway, Cheryl had a multitude of new bruises and a killer headache.

He opened the trunk.

"Get out!" he ordered.

She sat up and tried to get her bearings. She was dizzy and had been hot for too long. She leaned over the edge of the trunk and vomited.

"Don't you dare get that stuff on my car! Get out!" he shouted as he grabbed her arm and pulled her out of the trunk. Her battered body fell to the ground.

She lay there unable to move. She was going into shock. Her mind was unable to cope, so her thoughts wandered back to Curtis.

"Darling, what's wrong?" Curtis softly asked. "You don't look like you feel well."

Cheryl looked into his loving eyes and said, "I'm not feeling too good. My body is achy and I'm running a fever. I think I have the flu, Honey. Don't get too close. I don't want you getting sick, too."

He scooped her out of the bed and carried her to the sofa. He gently laid her down and put a couple of pillows under her head. He spread the throw blanket over her, then walked to the kitchen. She could hear the sound of ice cubes clinking in a cup. Then she heard the sound of soda being poured. He opened the cupboard and rifled around. Then he came back to her, arms loaded with cold soda, crackers, tissues, and flu medicine.

"Oh, Honey... you're so good to me. I love you, Curtis. With every fiber of my being, I love you," she said with tears in her eyes.

"My Love, I would give everything I have for you. I love you from the deepest part of my soul, Cheryl. You lay here and sip your soda and snack on crackers. Get some food in your tummy before you take the meds. While you're doing that, I'll find the TV remote. Might as well watch some gameshows while you're resting."

She had faded into unconsciousness as her mind focused on Curtis.

"Love? My Love? Honey, wake up. There's work to do. You have to wake up," Curtis said.

Her eyelids fluttered open and then she closed them again. She was aware of what was happening. Pete was dragging her into the house.

"He's not taking me to the cellar this time... what's he going to do with me?"

He tossed her on the living room floor and slammed the door behind him. He turned to face the door. She heard the deadbolt click.

"Cheryl, Cheryl, Cheryl," he said as he began to pace. "What am I going to do with such an unruly wife? I give you a beautiful home, a lovely lawn, and all the bills get paid. What do I get in return? A wife who is constantly trying to ruin my reputation. When I chose to marry you, I thought I was getting a loving, supportive wife. But that's not at all what I got. You're a problem, Cheryl. You've got to learn your lesson. It turns out I'm good at helping people learn lessons. I'm a teacher after all."

He walked into the home office. Cheryl heard loud shuffling from the room. After a few minutes, he came back into the living room and grabbed her leg. He dragged her to the office and then let go.

"Get up!" he ordered.

She used the desk chair for support as she got to her feet. Her head was swimmy, and she still felt nauseated.

"Into the closet!" he demanded.

Cheryl looked where he was pointing.

"Get in!" he shouted.

Cheryl cautiously walked to the closet and stepped inside, stumbling over boxes as she turned to face her husband.

"By the way, how is that spider bite doing?" Pete mockingly asked as he closed the door and locked it.

"His office closet has a lock?" she thought.

She was out of steam, so she sat on one of the boxes in the closet floor. She heard Pete's laughter as he exited the room and shut the office door behind him.

"At least I'm in the house this time and not in that smelly cellar. Maybe I can get some rest while I'm locked up."

She leaned her head against the wall and closed her eyes. She heard him working on the bathroom door, trying to get it unlocked. She heard him shut off the shower she had left running earlier that morning. The next sound was that of the TV. She was sure he was kicked back in his recliner, probably having a snack. That's ok. She didn't care. As long as he was away from her.

As the hours passed, she drifted in and out of sleep. Her thoughts went to Curtis.

"Oh, how I miss him!" she whispered. Tears began to roll down her cheeks. She was strong and resilient, but Pete's abuse was wearing her down. So, she cried. She let herself grieve her husband, and she let herself grieve for herself and the life she was losing to Pete. As she sat there and sniffled in the silence, she heard Pete's sickening laughter from the living room.

"I've got to get ahold of myself. Stop crying, Cheryl. There has to be a way to get out of here. Think, girl!" she whispered to herself.

She looked around in the darkness. Her eyes had adjusted, and she could see boxes stacked in a corner. She slid the top one off the stack and sat it on the floor next to her. There was a smidge of light coming in around the cracks of the closet door, so she opened the box and looked inside. It was filled with notebooks.

"BARBARA," she mouthed as she read the cover of the notebook on top. She dug through the stack. All were labeled with Barbara's name. "His second wife was named Barbara," Cheryl whispered to herself.

She took the lid off the next box. It was filled with tax receipts and paperwork from the past several years. So were the next two boxes she looked at.

She had reached the bottom of the stack of boxes before she realized she was sitting on one. She took off the lid and found another stash of notebooks.

"JILLIAN," she read as she dug through them. "They're all labeled with Jillian's name. She was his first wife."

Cheryl could still hear the sound of the TV playing in the living room, but she hadn't heard a peep out of Pete in several minutes. In the seclusion of the closet, she opened one of the notebooks labeled Barbara.

"I don't know what's going on with Barbara lately," she read. "She stumbles a lot and can't seem to keep her balance. Yesterday, I found her lying at the bottom of the cellar steps. I helped her up the steps and into the house. I had her sit down while I cleaned her up and dressed her wounds."

"Who is writing this? It's obviously not Barbara. Did Pete write this?" Cheryl wondered.

She continued reading.

"Just when her wounds were almost healed, Barbara fell on the patio and bruised her forehead. I just don't know what's going on with her. I've told her and told her she needs to see the doctor, but she refuses. There's nothing I can do," it read.

The next day's entry said, "I've tried to get Barbara to start taking her heart medicine again, but she refuses. She says she doesn't like taking medicine and she's sure her heart is fine. Her ankles and face are swollen. I think she's retaining fluid. But she still refuses to take her medicine."

Cheryl was puzzled. Was Pete documenting these things? Why? He wasn't documenting the great times they had, like vacations or parties. He was only journaling about her ailments and how she kept getting hurt and refusing meds.

She grabbed another notebook from the stack and read further, "My sweet, sweet Barbara is bedridden now. Her body is swollen and bruised. It's been weeks since she's taken her heart medicine. I'm afraid her heart is failing, but she doesn't want to see a doctor. She wants to die peacefully at home. Oh, my precious Barbara! Five months of marriage hasn't been long enough. I will love you until the day I die!"

With the faintest of light to read by, Cheryl continued poring over page after page about poor Barbara. It was all the same. All the entries documented her refusal to take her meds and how her body was failing. She read every entry, until the final one.

"Barbara, my love, I will miss you. Your poor body is so bruised and battered from all of the falls you've taken lately. Your legs and face have been so puffy from fluid retention. You hardly look like yourself anymore, Darling. My precious Barbara, your heart gave up today, but my heart will never give up on you."

"Oh… he's leaving a paper trail to prove his innocence…" Cheryl thought. "When Barbara died, it must have looked like she was having problems with balance and falling down. And, based on the entries in this notebook, it would appear as though her death had possibly been caused by a heart issue because she refused to take her medicine. It's starting to make sense!"

Disturbing as it was, she picked up a notebook with Jillian's name on the cover. Hers was a different story.

"Jillian went into a rage today. She threw a book at me when I walked in the door after work. She accused me of having an affair. Her mind is working overtime lately. She's become paranoid. I think she's going crazy. I may have to take her to the doctor if this continues."

The next entry read, "She accuses me of trying to kill her so I can marry someone else. She swears I have a mistress. I've told her repeatedly that I'm at work all day. I'm not seeing anyone. I always come home immediately after work. But she continues to accuse me. I'm afraid she's going to hurt me. Last night, I felt her get out of bed. I kept my eyes shut, but I stayed awake and listened. I heard her rummaging in the kitchen. I snuck down the hallway and rounded the corner to see her sorting through the knife drawer. She smiled at me and slid the drawer shut. I'm afraid she has bad plans for me."

"What on earth..." Cheryl muttered. "Was Jillian crazy?"

"I'm taking Jillian to have her assessed by a psychologist today. She's not in her right mind. I have no idea what could have pushed her to this point," he wrote. "My good friend Dr. Brant will have her ironed out soon. I'm sure of it. Hopefully, he will at least have her medicated by this weekend so he and I can keep our golfing plans."

Cheryl thought about all she had read. If Pete treated Jillian the same way he was treating Cheryl, of course the poor woman went crazy! And Barbara... he killed her. Cheryl had no doubt he killed his wife. She needed to read more so she picked up another notebook.

"Took Jillian to see Dr. Brant again yesterday. He said she's schizophrenic and a psychopath. He said she's a danger to me and I should have her institutionalized. He said if I don't lock her up, she could kill me. But I don't want to do that to my wife. I promised to love her and cherish her when we got married three months ago. I won't fail her. I will care for her until my dying day."

Notebook after notebook chronicled the life of crazy Jillian, until the last page.

"She came at me with a knife today. I walked in from work, and she ran at me with one of the carving knives in her hand. She was screaming that she would kill me for cheating on her. I told her repeatedly that she was my only love, but she didn't believe me. She tried to stab me with the knife. I stumbled backwards and she came at me again. So much screaming. She tried to stab me again. I shouted for her to stop, but she had gone mad. I grabbed the knife and wrenched it from her hand. She began to beat me with her fists. I held my hands up to defend myself. The knife was in my hand. I don't know how it happened, but somehow she impaled herself on it. My poor Jillian! The cops and coroner are on their way over now."

Cheryl wept as she read what happened. She couldn't help but to believe Pete had killed her deliberately. His journal entry made it look like he loved his wife, but Cheryl had seen how quickly he lied to cover up his wrongdoings. He had told Mr. Jacobs Cheryl had mental problems and was off her meds. That's how he explained her attempt to escape. He called his boss at the school and told her he would be late to work because his wife was sick, when the truth was he had her in the trunk of the car and was taking her home to punish her.

Everything Pete said was a lie. He killed both of them. He killed his wives.

She had no doubt she would be next.

Chapter 23

"He's not going to wait for my bruises and scrapes to heal. He'll just explain it away in a journal labeled 'Cheryl'," she realized as chills crept down her spine.

"What I don't understand is why. Why is he doing this? What could he have to gain by killing his wives? There's got to be some logic to this," she thought.

She grabbed one of the tax boxes and started perusing its contents in depth.

"Regular tax stuff," she said as she reached the bottom. "Let's see what's in the next tax box."

She removed the lid and started digging. She visually scanned document after document. Everything looked boringly normal. Until she reached a manila envelope labeled "banking". She opened it and read through the contents.

"Oh... when Barbara died, he automatically inherited what was in her bank accounts. They were married, so it naturally went to him," she whispered, not believing what she was seeing.

She continued digging and found evidence that he had also acquired Jillian's money. Neither woman had been a millionaire, but they'd both left Pete with sizable amounts.

"He probably couldn't collect all of their money. Their marriages were too short. But he obviously collected a large portion of it," she whispered to herself. "A very large portion. Enough to comfortably live on for the rest of his life, even without his teaching income."

She tucked the paperwork back into place and stacked the boxes back in the way she'd found them. She stood up. She'd been sitting for way too long.

"Bless my poor ankles! My legs and feet are so swollen. It's beginning to hurt. I really need my kidney medicine. It doesn't do any good to think about it, though. I don't have access to it… unless he hid it in this closet!"

She looked for more boxes on the floor, but she had already gone through all of them. Then she reached her hand up and felt along the high shelf of the closet. A shoe box, some loose papers, a pile of baseball caps, a notebook.

She squeezed and pressed the mound of baseball caps, hoping to feel the silhouette of a pill bottle.

"Nope, not there," she thought.

Then she slid the shoe box down and set it on the floor.

"More of a boot box than a shoe box," she whispered as she stooped to open it. "Yep, those are Pete's good cowboy boots. He used to wear these when he'd take me out on dates. I don't think he's worn them since our honeymoon."

She thought back to their honeymoon. They'd gone to the next town over and stopped in at an inexpensive motel. Their room had smelled stale, as though it hadn't been used in a long time.

"It probably *hasn't* been used in years. We're the only people in this whole shabby complex aside from the construction guys a few doors down," she'd thought.

Neither of them was young anymore. They both tried to be frugal, making sure they didn't spend too much now, so they'd have plenty to live on in their upcoming years. It made sense to save a penny here and there. So, she didn't complain about how cheap the motel was or how bad the room smelled. She didn't even complain when she went into the bathroom and found the light on a five-minute timer switch.

"I guess I'll learn how to bathe fast. Otherwise, I'll be showering in the dark."

But she drew the line at sleeping on bedding that appeared to be unwashed and tainted with droplets of some kind of dark fluid.

Pete wanted to stay because the cost was reasonable, but Cheryl insisted they get a refund and find a nicer place to stay. At least some place clean.

"That's fine as long as you pay for it," he'd told her. "I budgeted for the inexpensive place. If we're staying some place nice, you'll have to foot the bill."

"Pete... do you have any money?" she'd tentatively asked. "I'm not complaining. I understand about being frugal. But to choose to stay in a motel that's absolutely nasty... are you broke?"

"Of course not!" he'd bellowed. "I am beyond set financially! But I don't want to waste my money on silly stuff! I treat my money as though it means something!"

"No need to get upset," she consoled. "I just thought it would be good to ask you about it. You know, we got married so fast that we never sat down to discuss finances."

She smiled, hoping to take some tension away from the moment.

"I'll pay for the room," she said. "Let's get out of here and find some place we actually *want* to stay in."

Cheryl chose a hotel that offered a continental breakfast. Their room was clean and smelled fresh. The bedding was washed and crisp, and the pillows were plump. They stayed at the hotel for two nights and went downstairs both mornings to enjoy the free breakfast.

The rest of their honeymoon consisted of... not much. They walked through town and did some window shopping. They browsed a candy shop where Cheryl purchased a small block of homemade orange cream fudge and a bag of freshly-popped kettle corn to munch on as they strolled.

"Pete, look at this beautiful furniture!" she said as they walked past a storefront filled with an array of elegant pieces. "We should buy new recliners and a sofa while we're on our honeymoon! When we get home to start our new life, we'd be starting it with a fresh living room set!"

Pete looked at the ground and had his hands tucked deeply into his pockets.

"No," he quietly said as he looked up, "marriage isn't a time to spend money. It's a time to make money grow."

"That's a new one for me," she sweetly smiled. "What does it mean? How can we use our marriage to make money grow?"

He stared at the leather armchair in the window. There was a fake fireplace next to it, a rug on the floor, and a plush toy dog sleeping in front of the flickering artificial fire.

"You see that little dog lying in front of the fire?" he asked in a solemn tone. "The dog is at rest. He isn't doing a thing. He's useless. Just something to look at and trip over. He's in the way. Just a mouth to feed. He's worthless, yet he enjoys the life his master provides."

"Ok..." Cheryl said, curious as to where he was going with his analogy.

"Where's the master?" he asked as he took his hand out of his pocket and pointed to the empty chair. "See, while the dog is enjoying the comfort of the home, the master is out making things happen. He has plans to increase his financial standing and he's working them out. The dog is merely a distraction."

Cheryl stood in silence, trying to make sense of what Pete said. She stared at him with a look of confusion on her face.

"You don't understand, do you?" he asked. "You aren't expected to. You just enjoy the life I provide for you. I'll take care of the rest."

She gently shook her head as if doing so would erase the memory of their odd honeymoon. She refocused herself on the box of boots she had placed on the floor.

"What am I doing?" she whispered to herself, having been lost in memory for several minutes. "Oh! I'm looking for my pills."

She opened the box and took one of the boots out. She turned it upside down and shook it. Nothing fell out. There was no pill bottle. She replaced it and repeated the process with the other boot. Still no pill bottle.

She slipped her fingertips inside the boot as she grasped it by the top of the shaft. As she moved to place it back in the box, she felt a sheet of paper slip beneath her fingers.

"What's this?" she muttered as she pulled the paper out of its hiding place.

It turned out to be several papers stapled together. So, she laid the boot back in the box and turned toward the door to hold the papers in the light. She leaned closer to the door, straining her eyes to see the print. She heard herself breathing.

"Cheryl, get ahold of yourself," she mentally scolded.

She heard the breathing again, but this time it wasn't coming from her.

She peered through the crack at the edge of the closet door and saw an eye staring back at her.

"Pete!" she internally shrieked.

"How's life in solitary, Sweetie?" he teased. "Getting lonely in there?"

She needed more time in the closet, so she decided to play his game.

In a weak voice, she said, "It's really lonely in here, Pete. I'm scared and thirsty. I'm suffering."

She had subconsciously crossed her fingers in hope as she spoke to him. It wasn't the same thing as a prayer, but it was as close as she could get in the moment.

His laughter was ugly. She could smell his rancid breath wafting into the closet. He walked away, leaving his wife behind. She didn't know how much time she had, so she immediately held the papers in the dim light and began to skim over them.

"These are documents he printed from the computer. They look old. The edges are yellowed from a combination of oily fingerprints and age. He must have looked at these papers a lot."

The first page contained what looked like recipes. Not food recipes. It looked like recipes for chemical concoctions. Nothing interesting enough to actually read, so she flipped to the second page.

"What's this handwriting along the edge?" she wondered as she strained her eyes. "Jillian!" she gasped. "It says Jillian!" She quickly thumbed through the remaining pages. "More writing... Barbara!" she excitedly whispered. And as she thumbed over to the back of the stack, she found her name too.

Chapter 24

She began reading the information beside her name, assuming this passage had something to do with her.

"A high-percentage hydrogen peroxide solution is required for this task," she mouthed as she silently read the document. *"Obtain a 30% or greater solution. Multiple gallons may be required for thorough execution of the job.*

"There is much to be done before opening the first jug. Begin in the utility room of the home. Place several dry cotton towels in the clothes dryer. Put a full load into the machine. Leave the dry towels there as they will help fuel the fire.

"Arrange a stack of neatly folded sheets, towels, and blankets (all of pure cotton, hemp, or linen fabric) on top of the dryer. The goal is to create the appearance that the laundry area has been in heavy use all day. You've been washing bedding, towels, etc.

"Place stacks of the same types of items on utility room shelving and in cabinets, giving the room an authentically useful appearance while also providing an abundance of fodder for fire.

"Next, go into the bedrooms and arrange messy piles of bedding, as though you were in the process of stripping dirty bedding and preparing to wash. You may also add throw pillows (cotton, hemp, or linen), standard bed pillows, and the occasional teddy bear (if such can be found in an organic, flammable material). Best placement of these piles is in a wood-frame chair near the entry door of the bedroom, if the chair appears to be in its natural environment there. This will allow air circulation above, around, and beneath the pile of bedding. Items should be loosely arranged for maximum air flow. If placing them in a chair isn't an option, floor placement will work.

"All windows should be adorned with flammable cotton (hemp, linen) draperies. Four panels per ordinary window is ideal. Window toppers, like valances, are encouraged.

"To further encourage fire, place a stack of old newspapers near the homeowner's easy chair. Place a pile of tax return documents on the dining table. Add a stockpile of rolls of paper towels and toilet tissue in bathrooms and in the utility room. If the home has shelves of books, make spaces between the volumes for air to circulate, increasing the chances of the pages igniting. Paper is your friend. Arrange as many paper products as possible in strategic locations throughout the house. Every home has such items. They will add fuel to the fire in a way that appears natural.

"Once all flammables are in place, return to the laundry room. You may now open your first container of hydrogen peroxide. Soak the towels you have placed in the dryer. All fabric needs to be damp but not dripping wet. The goal is for the water element of the peroxide to evaporate, allowing the remaining element of peroxide to spontaneously combust. The door of the dryer must be slightly open to allow evaporation and air flow, as well as to allow the flame to reach into other parts of the utility area.

"It is tempting to douse all other flammable fabrics in the house as well, but do not. The fire inspector only needs to see one source of ignition, and that will be the clothes dryer. The other flammables will catch fire easily enough on their own.

"As you prepare to leave the domicile, you shall open the utility room window six inches to allow fresh air into the house. You will then do the same with the window farthest away, presumably at the far end of the house. This will create a bit of a draft to encourage flame. If there is no window in the utility room, open the nearest window by six inches (cracking open an exterior door can be used as a last resort).

"Everything you have done looks natural. It's natural to wash and dry towels. It's natural to fold and store blankets and sheets in the laundry room. It's natural to have piles of dirty bed linens in bedrooms as they wait to be washed. It's natural to have drapes on windows.

"The hydrogen peroxide solution you use will break down in the heat of the blaze. The fire inspectors will see that the fire started in the dryer, but they won't be able to detect foul play.

"Be sure to take your empty peroxide containers with you and dispose of them promptly in such a way that they won't be found. Afterward, be seen in public, with friends or colleagues, witnesses to prove you were with them and away from the house when the fire started. There is no exact timeframe to estimate onset of combustion. It will likely take hours. Use your time wisely."

The information was a lot for Cheryl to take in.

"Why did he write my name beside that information?" she wondered. "Maybe I'd better see what he wrote Jillian's and Barbara's names beside." She thumbed back through the pages until she came to Barbara's name.

She skimmed the information, quickly stringing together fragments of what she was reading, and she came to a conclusion. Heart medicine, overdose, not traceable, autopsy.

"He used her heart medicine against her!" she whispered in a moment of revelation. "His journal says she refused to take her heart medicine, resulting in balance issues and all sorts of falls that caused her to appear battered. He probably pushed her into the cellar, dragged her across the yard, and did all of the same foul things as he's done to me! He probably withheld her heart medicine, hoping she would die of natural causes, and maybe that *is* why she died. Or maybe he gave her an overdose of her medicine, just like this paper describes! The medicine is prescribed to her, so that would look legitimate. And it says here that a mild overdose is nearly impossible for a coroner to detect, especially since it's her prescription and she's supposed to have it in her system! He must have used her own medication to kill her!"

She flipped back toward the beginning of the sheaf of papers.

"Ok, Crazy Jillian," she mouthed to herself. "What did he do to you?"

Her jaw dropped in disbelief as she began to read the paragraph beside Jillian's name.

"The ingestion of rapeseed oil can trigger the aging process, causing the body to deteriorate quickly. Tumors can arise, and the nervous system may be affected. Survivors of rapeseed oil poisoning may experience insanity. The oil, used for industrial purposes, is not meant for human consumption. To disguise the flavor, it may be cut with other types of cooking oil and added to foods."

The realization hit her like a ton of bricks. She was so shaken she had to put her hand on the closet wall for support.

"The man induced her insanity... that's why the doctor said she was crazy. She had schizophrenia... the doctor said she was a psychopath... Pete poisoned her! Oh, that poor woman!"

She began to weep and decided she had snooped enough. She didn't want to find anything else. Pete was awful, and he was in the next room. She carefully tucked the papers back inside the boot and silently slid the box into its place on the shelf. As she released the box, her hand brushed against the notebook she had noticed earlier.

"Another notebook!" she gasped. "I was so focused on finding my pills earlier that I didn't pay any attention to it." She pulled it from the shelf and held it near the light at the edge of the closet door. There was writing on the cover.

"CHERYL"

"He's already started my journal!" she frantically whispered.

As she was about to flip open the notebook, she heard the sound of the office door. She hurriedly slid the notebook back onto the shelf and stood facing the closet door waiting to be let out.

She heard the lock click. Pete swung the door wide.

"How are you doing, Baby? Is it lonely in there? Truly, Cheryl, I don't understand why you keep doing this to yourself," he said with a smirk. "Tell you what, why don't you go into the kitchen and work on cooking a really delicious meal. We'll pretend I didn't find you in the trunk of my car earlier? Doesn't that sound good?"

Something shifted in Cheryl's spirit. She was tired of playing defense. She would play his game. The only difference would be a shift of power.

"Yes," she said with an artificially trembling voice. "I would like to do that."

Pete stared into her eyes, his hot nasal breath blowing into her face.

"I want to.. to do that..." she stammered, coaxing him into a false sense of power. You.. you should relax.. and enjoy some time on the patio. I'll cook us the most amazing meal you've ever tasted," she said.

She slumped her shoulders as though she had succumbed to his omnipotence and quietly led the way out of the room. Pete puffed out his chest and then followed. Cheryl went to the kitchen and started getting pots and pans ready for meal preparation. Pete walked past the kitchen to the patio, staring at Cheryl, confident that he had her right where he wanted her. He slid the glass door open and went outside.

"Oh, yes, Honey," she muttered in a venomous whisper. "You're so powerful and strong. I'm weak. I'm nothing. I'm at your mercy." She chuckled as she grabbed her cookbook and began thumbing through recipes. "Oh, Pete, this will be a meal to die for."

Chapter 25

She glanced out the kitchen window. Pete was sitting in his patio chair, watching videos on his phone. Cheryl turned back to the task at hand.

"He plans to burn me!" she fumed. "His stupid documents... he plans to set the house on fire and burn me with it!"

She flung open the medicine cabinet. Antihistamine, and plenty of it. An old bottle of prescription narcotics from when Pete had knee surgery last year. A full bottle of aspirin.

"That should do it," she whispered to herself.

She put a kettle of water on the stove so she could make sweet tea. While the water was warming, she heated a skillet and started sautéing onions and bell peppers. When the kettle whistled, she took it off the stove, poured it into a ceramic pitcher and added six tea bags. She wanted the tea to be strong and sweet, so when she took the bags out, she added a cup and a half of sugar. She stirred it until the sugar dissolved.

"What do I want to add to the tea?" she thought as she looked in the cabinet again. I think the prescription pain medicine will be a good start."

She touched one of the pills to her tongue. It was slightly bitter.

"Yes, this one will work perfectly in the tea," she said to herself. She added 10 tablets to the hot tea and stirred until they had dissolved. She scooped a drop of tea into a spoon and tasted it.

"Just a hint of bitterness, but it's not too much. I'll add a squeeze of lemon. That should take the edge off of the flavor."

With lemon added, the tea was ready.

Back at the stove, she added ground beef to the hot skillet and browned it while stirring in the sautéed vegetables. She added a can of cream of mushroom soup and mixed it all together. Then she reached into the spice cabinet for garlic, celery, and onion powders.

As she seasoned the food, she mumbled, "How about a dose of antihistamine to ward off Pete's seasonal allergies?" The bottle was only half full. "Well, I'll just use them all," she thought, as she emptied the container of capsules into the hot dish. She tossed the empty bottle in the trash and then stirred the meat and antihistamine mixture for several minutes. Once there was no trace of the capsules remaining, she dumped it all into a casserole dish. Using a clean spoon, she dipped the tiniest morsel from the dish and tasted it.

"I can't tell there's anything odd in it at all. Wonderful!"

"Between the narcotics in the tea and the allergy medicine in the casserole, Pete is sure to need a long, solid nap after dinner."

She topped the entrée with a heavy hand of shredded cheese and then popped the dish in the oven.

While it baked, she added two cans of pork and beans to the skillet that was still hot. She stirred in garlic powder, a dash of powdered cayenne, some ketchup, molasses and a squeeze of mustard. After stirring it all together, she put in a dollop of bacon drippings to give it a smoky flavor.

"Time for some aspirin," she mumbled, as she poured several tablets into her hand. She warmed a mug of water in the microwave to dissolve the tablets. Once all the pills had disappeared, she stirred the tainted water into the beans.

"I already know aspirin tastes bitter. How can I mask the flavor? Hmmm... maybe a dash of lemon will soften the bitterness here too. She grabbed another fresh lemon, halved it, and then squeezed every drop of juice into the beans.

She gave it a good stir and checked the flavor.

"Wow! Baked beans are actually good with added lemon. I'll have to remember this in the future! I just have to make sure I have a future..."

Then she poured the beans into another dish and added it to the hot oven.

She steamed some wild rice to round out the meal, and then she whipped up some chocolate chip cookies, with a sprinkle of pulverized aspirin tablets blended into the dough for added oomph. With everything removed from the oven, the meal was ready.

"This, dear Cheryl, is a special occasion. Let's use the China plates tonight," she told herself with a smile. She set the table with the prettiest plates and the good silverware. She placed the dishes of food on the table and filled the tea glasses with ice.

"Wait!" she whispered in a panic. "What am I going to eat? I didn't save any unmedicated food for myself!"

She quickly grabbed a can of beans from the cabinet and dumped a portion onto her dinner plate. Then she added a large scoop of rice to make her plate look full.

"That should be good enough to keep from rousing suspicion."

She stuck her head out the patio door.

"Dinner's ready, Darling," she said.

He didn't respond, but she knew he would be in soon. The food smelled delicious. There's no way he could resist for long.

She grabbed his plate and piled it high with beans. Then she made a bed of wild rice, but not too much rice. She didn't want him to fill up on the one food she didn't doctor. Then she topped the rice with a large spoonful of the creamy meat dish. Then she added another spoonful, and another.

She poured Pete's glass full of tea and added a wedge of lemon to the glass. Then she sat in her chair at the dining table and waited.

She heard the door slide open and Pete came inside. He went to the bathroom to wash up, then came back and seated himself.

He took a long drink of tea, then sat the glass down and began to shovel food into his mouth. Cheryl was satisfied to see her husband enjoying his dinner.

She ate tiny bites of her food so he wouldn't get suspicious, but she wasn't the least bit hungry. She wouldn't be hungry again until her plan came to fruition and she was free.

Every time Pete's tea glass started to get low, Cheryl popped a few more ice cubes in it and topped it off with her special sweet tea. When she started to see the bottom of his plate, she replenished his food with big dollops of her extra-special concoctions.

Finally, he pushed back his plate and said he was done.

"You can't be done yet," Cheryl cooed. "I made cookies. You have to have a couple of cookies to make the meal complete."

She grabbed the plate of cookies from the kitchen counter and set them in front of Pete. She picked up three of them and laid them on the edge of his plate. Pete had a sweet tooth. She knew he'd eat all three, even though his stomach was already full.

She topped off his tea glass again and said, "I'll start cleaning up the dishes. You go enjoy some TV and relax."

He scooted his chair back from the table and made a beeline for his recliner.

"Hmmm, he looks a little sleepy to me," Cheryl thought with satisfaction.

She washed their dinnerware and wiped down the kitchen. She carried the dishes of food from the table and placed them on the kitchen counter. Wondering what to do with the contaminated food, she decided to check Pete's current condition.

She peeked around the corner and saw him. He was completely unconscious, TV gently roaring in the background.

"Yeah, I think this food has gone bad. I'd better throw it out," she happily whispered as she dumped it all in the trash can. "I won't worry about anyone finding it. The fire will be hot enough to burn all the evidence."

Chapter 26

"Time to light some candles. This house needs a little ambiance," she softly said as she walked throughout the house gathering every candle they owned. She placed them all around the living room, with most of them near Pete's chair.

"His resting place," she chuckled.

She lit the candles and let them flicker while she went to the office. She sat down in the rolley chair and opened Pete's laptop. Then she went to his personal emails.

She clicked the 'Compose' icon and began an email. In the 'To' box, she added every person in Pete's contacts. In the subject line, she typed *"I'm not what I seem"*.

She began typing the body of the email.

To Whom it May Concern,

I have failed you. I'm not the man you believe me to be. I'm not a good man. I'm a man who does bad things. I killed my wives. All three of them. Well, I think Cheryl is dead. I'm not sure. I beat her and left her body in the storm cellar out back. If you check my bank account, you will see I have large deposits from when I killed Barbara and Jillian. Since they were my wives and had no other heirs, their money automatically went to me. How did this happen to me? How did I become a monster? I'm going to kill myself. I don't deserve to live. I've done very bad things.

Pete Adams

"Send," Cheryl whispered as she hit the button.

She copied the sent message, then went to Pete's school and police reserves emails. She pasted his farewell message and sent it to everyone in his contacts list for both accounts.

"Now, everyone associated with Pete through work or the police reserves will know who he really is. Nothing will be left in the dark."

She walked back to the living room where Pete was heavily sedated.

"Now that his reputation has been brought to light," she muttered to herself, "I think it's time to bring some other things to light, like this house."

She stood in the living room, listening to Pete's raspy breathing. She was thinking about what she would do next when his phone rang!

She jumped and gasped.

"Where's his phone?!"

It rang a second time and a third. She tracked it to the side pocket of his cargo pants. She had to retrieve it and turn it off before the noise woke him.

She gently pulled the pocket open, the hook-and-loop closure making a loud noise as she did, and she slipped her hand inside, grasping the phone as it rang again.

She flicked it to silent mode, then looked to see who was calling. It was one of Pete's friends, one he went fishing with on a regular basis. The call switched to voicemail, and the transcription appeared on the screen.

"Pete, man, what's going on? What's up with that email? Is this a prank? Call me, man. I mean it. No, forget that. I'm coming over. Don't you dare do something stupid."

Cheryl was pleased that his friend had read the email. She smiled as she read the transcription a second time. Then she realized she shouldn't be standing there.

"I've got to get moving before people show up to check on him! Why am I standing here like I have all the time in the world?" she whispered in a panic.

His phone screen lit up again as she laid it on the table beside him. Another call from a worried acquaintance.

"How can I keep him from waking up and escaping when the flames hit him?" she thought. "Maybe I could tie him to the chair... and the rope would burn off and probably vaporize in the extreme heat. There would be no evidence that he was tied. That's what I'll do."

She ran to the utility room and checked the tool cabinet. She found a roll of hemp twine. She grabbed a pair of pruning shears and took her supplies to the living room.

Pete's breathing was shallow. He wasn't moving.

Cheryl quickly cut a long length of twine and wrapped it twice all the way around Pete's legs and the footrest of the recliner. Then she cut a much longer piece of string and wrapped it around his torso and the backrest of the chair.

"His hands should be bound too. Otherwise, he might be able to untie the other strings," she thought as she cut another long piece of twine. She wrapped it around his left wrist multiple times and tied it to the leg of the end table beside his chair. She wrapped his right wrist the same way and tied the twine to the leg of the bookshelf at the other side of the recliner.

"There," she said. "That should do it."

She grabbed a couple of water bottles from the kitchen and filled them with tap water. Then she snagged granola bars from the cupboard. She placed her refreshments by the front door.

"It's time," she softly said as she looked at Pete. He didn't seem so evil as he lay there in deep slumber. But she knew the man he was. A man like him shouldn't be allowed to live. The final killing in Pete's life had to be his own.

She arranged the flaming jar candles along the bookshelf near his chair. She made a cluster of them on the end table. Then she moved one just a smidge too close to the curtain. It caught fire.

"Oh, my," Cheryl said. "Tsk, tsk," she whispered. "We shouldn't burn candles so close to the drapes, should we, Pete?"

She grabbed another candle and placed it on the floor at the base of his chair. She tilted it at an angle so it would look as if the jar had fallen from the bookshelf. It would look natural, as she was sure there would soon be quite a chaotic scene where Pete was sleeping.

The skirt of his chair started to smolder. Then it began to melt and drip to the floor. The hotter it got, the more smoke it made.

"Come on, fire! Don't let me down!" she encouraged. "You've got to catch flame. I can't just smoke him to death."

Just then the fabric of the chair caught fire. Droplets of the melting fabric hit the carpeted floor in tiny blazes. Her plan was coming together.

She hunkered low to stay below the smoke line. The house was rapidly filling with fumes. She ran to the door, grabbed her food and water, and stepped outside. As she did, she remembered she needed Pete's car keys, so she reached back in and found them hanging from the hook. Her body was shaking with adrenaline as she twisted the lock on the door and pulled it shut.

She glanced at the window. The curtains were being consumed by flames. She smiled as she turned and raced toward Pete's car.

She knew if she stole it, her plan wouldn't work. The cops would be on the lookout for whoever took the car, assuming the bandit would be responsible for the housefire.

She opened the driver's side door and cranked the car. Then she backed it down the driveway to get it away from the house. She didn't want the car to get too hot when the house became engulfed in flames.

She moved it to an area that looked like a normal place to park. She was comfortable with her distance from the house. She popped the trunk and then walked to her hiding spot. She tossed her water inside, threw in her snacks, and was about to add herself to the compartment when she paused. She took one last glance at the house. Thick smoke billowed behind the windows. It poured from the vents at each end of the attic.

She heard small explosions from inside the house. And then a muted roaring noise. The roar trembled and then grew louder and higher in pitch.

It was a throaty scream.

Pete was awake.

There was another explosion. She turned her head away and shielded her eyes. When she looked back toward the house, she saw the living room windows had shattered. She watched as flames reached out like greedy hands looking for more. The roof of the porch was catching fire. Rolling flames billowed from the attic vents. The sight made her feel sick.

The fire created a scorching wind that set the trees at the edges of the yard into a frenzied dance. Some of the branches emitted steam as they were seared. Others smoldered with leaves bursting into miniature flames.

Their home, what Cheryl had expected to be a safe haven in their marriage, was now a scene of utter chaos.

She heard a car approaching. She quickly shut the trunk, sequestering herself inside. She listened intently. The car passed by. She heard it stop and reverse. The driver parked in the road.

"Yes, I need to report a fire. A house is on fire," a man's voice said. "I don't know the address. It's Pete Adams's house. His car is still here. He must be inside. I'm going to see if I can help him!"

"Oh!" Cheryl gasped. She hadn't thought about the possibility of innocent people getting hurt. She wanted to jump out of the trunk and scream, "No! Let him die!" but she knew she had to remain silent. Otherwise, the whole plan would be a waste, and she'd probably end up in prison.

It was only a matter of minutes until she heard the sound of sirens. Lots of them. She heard emergency vehicles pulling onto the lawn and parking alongside the road. She heard voices shouting and equipment clanging. The rescue was in full swing. She just had to wait it out.

It was getting hot in the trunk. She gulped water. She opened a granola bar, but she couldn't eat it. She was too upset to be hungry. She lay on the floor with sweat pouring off of her. The spider bite stung terribly in the salty sweat of her neck, but she hardly noticed. Her thoughts were focused on the condition of the house.

"It should be fully engulfed in flames by now," she thought. Pete would be dead. A wave of nausea washed over Cheryl. She curled up into a loose fetal position and closed her eyes, listening to the loud crackle of the house burning and the firemen trying to rescue Pete.

But she knew it was too late for him to be saved. Her plan was becoming reality. It was sickeningly perfect.

"Once the firemen and cops leave tonight, I'll go into the woods and conveniently wander out when they come back to investigate the fire tomorrow. I will look the part for sure. I'm a mess, scrapes and bruises all over. That should work. I will tell them I escaped from the storm cellar and didn't know where to go because I was addled."

She heard more vehicles pull up, more voices. And then the sound of a woman screaming.

"Cheryl's in there!" the woman screamed. "My friend is in there! Get her out!"

"Is that... Lorraine?" Cheryl whispered.

"Get out of my way!" the woman screamed.

"That *is* Lorraine!" Cheryl realized. "No, Lorraine, don't go in! Please don't go in!" she whispered to herself.

She heard a man's commanding voice saying, "Ma'am! Ma'am! It's too late! No one in that house has survived. I'm so sorry."

Cheryl slowly opened the trunk just enough to see out. Evening was coming on. It was dusky dark outside. She could see Lorraine being comforted by a fireman.

"I'm so sorry, Lorraine," Cheryl whispered in the solitude of the trunk. "I'm so sorry you're having to go through this. But it's the only way."

She continued to watch the events around her from the trunk of the car. She couldn't see the house from her vantage point, but she was able to people watch. Everyone's focus was on the house and firefighting equipment. It was time.

"Where's Lorraine's car?" she thought as she took in all of the vehicles parked in front of her yard. "There it is!"

She took one last gulp of water, then quietly eased out of her hiding spot. It was dark enough now that no one would notice her.

She softly closed the trunk and pressed down hard to be sure it latched itself closed. Then she skulked to the nearest vehicle and darted to the next and then the next. And then to Lorraine's.

"Please don't be locked," she muttered as she tried the rear door. It opened and Cheryl slipped inside.

"Darn interior light!" she muttered as she quickly pulled the door closed behind her and crumpled into a ball on the floor. Lorraine's jacket was in the back seat, so Cheryl pulled it over the top of her to conceal herself.

Hours passed. Cheryl ached from lying on the floor, but she dared not move.

Then the driver's door opened, and she felt the car jostle as Lorraine sat down. She shut the door and began crying. She mourned for several minutes. She cried so hard for so long that it sounded as though she couldn't breathe anymore. Cheryl's heart was breaking for her friend, but she couldn't risk revealing herself yet. She needed to get away from the scene of the crime. She needed to get away from Pete, the house, and all of his friends who had come to rescue him. She needed to be completely alone with Lorraine when she revealed herself.

Finally, Lorraine cranked the car and began to drive.

"Why, God? Why did you let something like this happen to someone so precious?" Lorraine prayed aloud in the privacy of her car. "Cheryl is such a loving, kind person. Why did you let Pete do this to her? Why didn't you stop him?" She began crying again. She reached for her purse to get a tissue. "Oh, good grief," she said. "I can't see through my tears. I'm going to have to pull over and get myself together enough to be able to drive home. Where are my tissues?" she muttered as she rifled through her purse with one hand and steered the car into an empty parking lot with the other. "Oh, I think I have one in my jacket pocket."

She shifted the car into park and turned to retrieve her jacket from the backseat. "How'd it get in the floor?" she questioned.

She pulled her jacket to her without noticing Cheryl lying there. It was dark and her eyes were blurred with tears. She took no notice.

"Should I tell her I'm here?" Cheryl thought. "There might be security cameras watching this parking lot. I'd better wait until we get to her house."

Lorraine blew her nose, dried her tears, and started driving again. A few minutes passed and Cheryl felt the car pull into the driveway. She glanced up and out the window and saw the great oak tree in Lorraine's yard.

She heard Lorraine remove her seatbelt. She knew she needed to say something before she got out of the car. She was afraid Lorraine would scream, and she didn't want the neighbors to hear.

"Lorraine?" Cheryl softly spoke.

Lorraine screamed and turned in her seat. She screamed again and began blindly beating whoever was in the back seat.

"Lorraine! It's Cheryl! Stop hitting me!" Cheryl said as she held her arms in front of her face.

Lorraine recoiled, and responded, "What?! What did you say?!"

"It's me. I'm ok. Well, I'm not ok. But I'm here and I'm not dead."

"Cheryl! You're not dead! Why did you do that to me?!" Lorraine squeaked as her voice cracked.

She reached back to hug her friend, and she began crying all over again.

"I had to, my sweet friend," Cheryl said. "I didn't want to, but I *had* to."

Chapter 27

Once they were in the house, Lorraine checked all the doors and windows to be sure they were locked. She closed the blinds and drapes, and she dimmed the lights. Then she sat Cheryl down and asked her what was going on.

"There's a lot that's going on," Cheryl responded. "I'm going to tell you all about it, but could I get a shower first? I feel disgusting."

"Of course," Lorraine said. "Let me put some fresh towels in the bathroom. Oh, and you'll need something to wear. Go ahead and start your shower. I'll pop in with clean clothes in a minute."

Cheryl made her way to the guest bath and started the shower. She let her clothes fall to the floor, then she glanced in the mirror.

"Oh my..." she moaned. "I'm so pale and swollen. My face is so puffy. And that spider bite... my whole neck is streaked with red."

She turned and stepped into the steamy shower. Lorraine knocked, then stepped in with her delivery of clean clothes.

"I wasn't sure if you needed pajamas and a robe, or if you needed getting-out-of-town clothes, so I brought both," Lorraine told her from the other side of the shower curtain.

"Thank you," Cheryl replied.

She enjoyed a long, soaking shower. When she stepped out onto Lorraine's plush bath rug, she felt exhausted yet refreshed.

She dressed in the pajamas and robe and walked to the living room. Lorraine was sitting in the rocking chair and waiting. Cheryl sat on the sofa across from her.

Lorraine handed her a bottle of apple juice and a plate of lemon cookies.

"Ok, spill," Lorraine said. "Tell me what happened. All of it. Leave nothing out."

Cheryl recounted the story of how she'd found Pete's journals masking the murder of his wives. She told how Pete dragged her across the yard and threw her in the cellar, how he'd locked her in the closet, how he'd stolen her car keys and her kidney medicine. She explained how she'd induced a deep sleep and lit the candles all around him. She told of how she'd sent the emails, and how she'd hid in the trunk listening to the commotion.

Lorraine's mouth was hanging open. She sat back in her chair, eyes as big as saucers.

"Why did you kill him, though? Couldn't you have escaped another way?" Lorraine asked, appalled at what her sweet friend had done. "Cheryl, you murdered him!"

She was taken aback by Lorraine's words, but she understood the response.

"Lorraine, I tried to escape. I wanted to call for help, but he destroyed my phone. I wanted to drive into town to see the doctor and get help, but he stole my car keys. I walked miles to the neighbor's house and called the police for help, but they called Pete, and he came and got me. I even hid in Pete's trunk and planned to get out and escape while he was at work, but he found me. He blocked me at every turn, Lorraine. And then I discovered the journals and read how he tried to make it look like his wives were responsible for their own deaths. Then I found the journal with my own name on it! Lorraine, he killed his wives! And I was next! I didn't know what else to do!"

"I'm sorry," Lorraine softy said. "I didn't mean to sound callous. I had no idea how bad it was. I got your letter this afternoon. I didn't take time to gather troops. I just jumped in my car and went to get you. But when I got there the house was up in flames. I thought you were gone. I thought I'd lost you!" she said as she began to cry. "I'm so glad you're ok!"

"I'm not entirely ok. I have an infected spider bite. Pretty sure it's brown recluse. I haven't been able to go to the doctor to get meds for it. And I haven't had my kidney medicine in days. I'm retaining fluid. I need my medicine. But now that everyone thinks I've died, I don't know how I can see a doctor or get my meds without the doctor's office alerting authorities that I'm alive."

Lorraine thought and then said, "I know! We'll go to another town far from here. You can see a new doctor and he can prescribe your medicine."

"Where can we go?" Cheryl questioned.

"It doesn't matter. Let's get in the car and start driving. You can't stay here anyway. Someone might find out you survived," Lorraine said. "Or do we want them to know you survived? What's your plan?"

"I'm not really sure. I just wanted to get away from Pete before he killed me, and I've done that. I'm afraid they will think I killed him if they find out I'm alive," Cheryl said.

"But, Honey, they're going to think that anyway when they don't find your body."

Chapter 28

They got in the car and started driving. It was well into the evening now and all the world was dark except for the occasional headlights they encountered on the road. They drove and talked, working toward figuring out the best route to take toward closure with the Pete situation.

"Cheryl, what if you wandered out from the woods around your house, dehydrated and filthy? What if a passerby found you wandering around? You could say Pete beat you and locked you in the cellar. You escaped when the house was on fire, and you wandered into the woods because you had lost your senses. And you've been wandering lost ever since. What do you think?"

"Actually, that was my original plan. I didn't foresee you coming to my rescue at the precise moment I needed you though. I really think it might work," Cheryl said, "but what if it doesn't? What if they suspect me of setting the house on fire? What if they send me to jail for what happened to Pete?"

"Think about it, Honey," Lorraine said. "Pete sent out a mass email telling everyone about the awful things he did. How he killed his wives, and he tried to kill you too. And he said he was going to kill himself. I don't think anyone will suspect you. The whole situation looks like Pete offed himself."

"Still, it makes me nervous. It could be a bad move to expose myself," Cheryl said.

"What's the alternative?" Lorraine asked. "You stay in hiding for the rest of your life, in fear every moment that the law will find you? That's no way to live, Cheryl."

"I suppose you're right. How will we do this? I really don't want to be left in the woods alone," Cheryl said.

"Let's see... it's after midnight now. There will be investigators all over the place tomorrow. How about I drop you off by the roadside early tomorrow morning while it's still dark and let you walk into the woods? Take a couple of hours to walk and work your way close to the yard and when you see investigators and cops show up to search through the rubbish, you can wander out of the woods acting injured and scared. I think that'll do it!" Lorraine exclaimed.

"I won't have to act. I *am* injured and scared! It sounds like it could work," Cheryl responded. "Do you think they will take me to a hospital?"

"I'm sure of it," Lorraine responded.

"Until then," Cheryl said, "how about we head back to your house and get some rest? I feel bad and need to shut my eyes for a bit."

Lorraine made a U-turn and headed for home. Both of them were exhausted, especially Cheryl. She spent what was left of the night in Lorraine's guest room, sound asleep on the soft mattress and feather pillows.

It was almost noon when they woke up. They'd slept much later than intended.

"Cheryl! Girl, wake up! We've got to get going!" Lorraine shouted as she shimmied out of her pajamas and into day clothes.

Cheryl sat upright in bed and checked the clock on the wall.

"Am I seeing that right? It's already noon?!" she muttered. "Where are the clothes I was wearing last night? I've got to put those grungy things back on!"

Lorraine shouted from her bedroom, "They're in the laundry room in the washer. I haven't washed them yet. They're still dry and filthy!"

Cheryl scrambled to get dressed. She slipped on her dirty shirt, jeans, and stiff socks. She had trouble with her shoes. Her feet were terribly swollen.

"What about my face and hair? Aside from my clothes, I don't look dirty at all," she mumbled to herself. Then she went to Lorraine's sun porch and scooped some potting soil from her philodendron pot. She rubbed the dirt all over her face and into her hair, mussing her locks in a frenzy.

She glanced at her reflection in the window. Satisfied with her appearance, she went into the kitchen for a glass of water. Lorraine rounded the corner and saw Cheryl in her glory of messiness. And she laughed. So hard that she doubled over. And then Cheryl laughed too, for the first time in a long time.

Lorraine secreted Cheryl to the car, tucking her under a blanket in the back floor. They began their drive to what would be Cheryl's freedom or her capture.

Cheryl began to sweat beneath the blanket. Not so much because she was hot, but because she was nervous and suddenly feeling quite ill.

"Lorraine, I think I need to stop. I'm feeling sick at my stomach," Cheryl said.

Lorraine pulled over about a mile from Cheryl's and Pete's burnt house.

"This is where you need to get out anyway," Lorraine said. "Do you think you can make it all the way back to the house?"

"I have no choice," Cheryl said. She quickly walked into the woods. Lorraine heard her retch and cough. Then silence. And then footsteps moving away from her.

"Good," Lorraine whispered to herself. "She's walking. She just has to make it to the house."

Lorraine drove toward Pete's house, curious what the place looked like this morning, and wondering if investigators were still there. She knew they would have started their work early this morning, but she didn't know how long it would take them.

As she approached the house, she saw several unmarked cars and two news vans.

"Oh my!" she whispered. "There are news crews here!"

She continued driving and then realized it would be ok if she stopped and got out of the car. This was her best friend's house, after all, so why shouldn't she stop and ask what investigators had discovered?

She pulled the car onto the grass at the edge of the lawn. She stepped out and looked for someone who appeared to be official. She spotted a woman in business khakis and a blue polo.

Lorraine approached and said, "Excuse me. My best friend lives here and I'm wondering if you can tell me what happened."

The woman gave Lorraine a look of compassion and said, "I'm sorry, but we aren't allowed to release any information at this time. It would be best if you go home. Any information we release will be on the news."

"Oh, I see," Lorraine replied. "It's just that she's my friend and I need to know if she survived or if she… passed."

A reporter overheard the conversation and approached Lorraine.

"Excuse me, Miss," he said. "Did I hear you say your friend lives here? Are you and Pete Adams well acquainted?"

"Pete Adams?!" Lorraine was shocked. "Not at all! My friend is Cheryl! Cheryl Adams! The wife Pete wanted dead!"

Reporters from both news stations gave Lorraine their full attention now. They fired a barrage of questions.

"I can use this to Cheryl's advantage," Lorraine thought. "I can get it on the news that Pete is an abuser and that he murdered his wives. It's already been sent in an email to everyone who knows Pete. Why not go ahead and get it on the news?"

She collected her thoughts and responded to their questions with a blanket answer.

"Pete is known and loved in this community. Everyone thinks he's an upstanding citizen. He's a school teacher for goodness sake!

"But he's not who he portrays himself to be. Cheryl confided in me that Pete keeps her secluded here in isolation. She's not allowed to be around other people because he's afraid she will tell them how he beats her and locks her in the cellar. He doesn't want her to have access to her medicine, so he hid it from her. He keeps her away from the rest of the world because he wants to kill her."

The reporters gasped and sputtered, "Why does she think this?" They held their microphones close to her in anticipation of a response.

"She believes he wants her to die so he can inherit her money," she coolly said. "It's what he did when he killed his other two wives, and it's what his plan is for her."

"Does she have proof?" one reporter asked.

Just as Lorraine was about to answer, she heard a commotion. Several of the investigators began jogging toward the woods.

"We found her! It's the wife!" they shouted.

The reporters forgot all about Lorraine and hauled their cameras and gear to the cluster of investigators that had gathered around Cheryl.

Lorraine smiled. It was all coming together. She called 911 and requested an ambulance, stating that Pete's abuse victim had just been discovered and she needed medical care. The more she could use the word 'abuse' in reference to Pete, the better. She wanted the town abuzz with news of Pete's maltreatment and murders.

She went over to Cheryl to join in the celebration of her discovery. She excitedly chatted with the investigators and news crews about the reappearance of the victim. And she hugged Cheryl like she hadn't seen her at all. No one had a clue she had spent the night in a comfortable bed at Lorraine's house.

Chapter 29

Six months later, Lorraine and Cheryl sat in the breakfast nook sipping hot tea together. Lorraine's home was quiet, cool, and the kind of place one never wanted to leave. Her walls were painted a soft shade of white, and each room was trimmed with a different color. The breakfast nook was accented by pale yellow trim.

The main feature of the little breakfast nook was the picture window that showcased the back yard patio. Lorraine had several bird feeders set up, and a colorful birdbath too. The two ladies sipped tea and watched the flurry of birds on the other side of the window, giggling every time one of Lorraine's resident squirrels scurried up to munch on seed that had fallen to the ground.

Her house had two bedrooms and two full baths. The master bedroom was decorated in bright colors and wild animal prints. It matched Lorraine's fun personality perfectly.

The guest room had a totally different vibe to it. Cheryl remembered when Lorraine had bought the house and moved in.

"Cheryl," she'd said, "this will be your room when we have girls' nights, and you want to crash here. How should we decorate it, Hon?"

"You mean I get to choose what this room will look like?" Cheryl had responded.

"Yep, this is your room, Hon! Do it up any way you want!"

Cheryl had thought about it for a couple of days before reaching a decision. Pink. She loved pink.

"Can we do the whole room in different shades of pink?" she asked Lorraine when she came over later in the week to help with unpacking.

"Absolutely!" she said. "Forget unpacking! Let's go to the paint store and look at colors!" she said as she grabbed her car keys and headed for the door.

So, Cheryl's room was painted in a soft blush and highlighted by fuchsia crown molding, window trim, and baseboards. The bed was topped with a handmade quilt Lorraine's sister had made from simple squares of cotton fabric in deep purple, hot pink, mauve, and rose with lavender borders. Four pillows, each in a different shade of pink, added an extra dose of color to the queen-sized bed.

She loved Lorraine's home. It was the most welcoming space she'd ever set foot in. When she was there, she was at peace.

An announcement from Lorraine brought her back to the moment.

"So," she said, "I've got a date Friday night!"

"You do?" Cheryl asked. "Well, tell me about him!"

Lorraine had only been back home from work for about half an hour, but even after a full day at the office, she looked vibrant and cheery. She had changed out of her work clothes and put on an elegant loungewear set, topped by a flowy, satin robe in a bold floral print. Her hair had been brushed and pulled into a messy bun that defied its name by being tidy. She was still wearing the day's jewelry. Earrings in the shape of hummingbirds, rings on each finger, and bangle bracelets that clanked and danced about on her arm with every movement as she told Cheryl about her upcoming date.

"I met him on a dating app. He's about my height, gray hair, a well-groomed beard and mustache, brown eyes, and it looks like he still has his own teeth!" she said with excitement.

Cheryl looked at her with a deadpan expression.

Lorraine asked, "What?"

Cheryl couldn't maintain her stoic appearance. She smiled, then giggled, then broke out in a fit of laughter that brought tears to her eyes. Which triggered Lorraine to laugh, and she didn't even know why she was laughing.

"You said he has his own teeth! Girl! Is that the bonus we're looking for these days?! Teeth?!"

The women got so tickled at the thought that they wheeze-laughed for several minutes before they were able to catch their breath.

Then Cheryl quietly said, "I'll never date again. I never want to get involved with anyone else. Curtis was the love of my life. He still is. There's no use in dating."

"Honey, don't give up on love. I know how much you and Curtis loved each other, but he's gone now. It's ok to meet someone new."

"Maybe, but the someone new I met nearly killed me," Cheryl responded.

"Girl, not everyone is like Pete. He was a one-of-a-kind mistake. I'm not saying most men are good. Actually, at our age, I think most men are just looking for someone that will take care of them. They're looking for a mother.

"But there are some men who are looking for a wife, someone to care for, to hold close at night, someone to love until eternity's end. Cheryl, it would do you good to get back out there."

"I think I'll pass," Cheryl said. "I'll play it safe and live vicariously through you, roomie."

The investigation into Pete and the fire left Cheryl looking innocent in the eyes of the law. She still felt fear every day, fear that her deeds would be brought to light. But, for now, what she had done was left in the darkness of the burned house along with Pete's ashes. The community believed her to be innocent. Pete had simply overdosed on medications in an attempt to commit suicide, and he'd left the candles burning, which had led to the fire.

Cheryl had moved in with Lorraine immediately after her discharge from the hospital. She was taking her kidney medicine daily and was no longer retaining fluid.

The emergency room had given her an IV of antibiotics to fight the infection from the spider bite. And they sent her home with loads of medicine. The bite had finally healed, but it left a noticeable scar that resembled a crater on her neck. It would forever be a reminder of what she had survived.

As Pete's widow, she had inherited his money. Her attorney searched, and found that Pete's parents and sister had died in a house fire when he was a kid. There was no one else to give the inheritance to, so every cent from his bank accounts now belonged to Cheryl. The money he had acquired from Jillian and Barbara was now in her hands. Every day she mentally debated on what to do with the money. Should she keep it and live on it for the rest of her days? She really didn't have to. She had plenty of money after Curtis's death. Should she give it to charity?

She wasn't sure how to handle it, so, for now, it was nestled securely in her savings account.

Chapter 30

The doorbell rang. Cheryl hopped up from her place at the kitchen table and walked over to answer it. It was a delivery driver.

"Hi, Cheryl," he said. "I have a package for you."

"I've been ordering a lot of packages lately!" she said with a smile. "I love shopping online and never having to leave the house!"

His hand brushed against hers as he handed her the box. She felt a rush of adrenaline.

"Stop it, Cheryl," she said to herself. "No more men."

"It's good to see you, Cheryl. You look especially lovely today," he said as he turned to go.

She blushed and then turned to go inside. Lorraine was standing within earshot. She had heard their interaction.

"Hmmm... no more men, you say?" Lorraine inquired with raised brow.

"Of course, no more men. And I mean it," Cheryl said as she set her package down and went online to place another order. "Definitely, no more men," she smiled as she hit the 'buy now' button.

Cheryl's story isn't over…

...neither is Pete's.

Made in the USA
Monee, IL
02 September 2025

24773336R00111